Mister Stormalong.   COPY 63

Malcolmson, Anne (Burnett) 1910–   J398.2
                                                      M
    Mister Stormalong, by Anne Malcolmson and Dell J. Mc-
Cormick. Illustrated by Joshua Tolford. Boston, Houghton Mifflin, 1952.

    136 p. illus. 24 cm.   2.75

Mister Stormalong

Mister Stormalong

BY
ANNE MALCOLMSON
AND ## DELL J. McCORMICK

ILLUSTRATED BY
JOSHUA TOLFORD

HOUGHTON MIFFLIN COMPANY, BOSTON
THE RIVERSIDE PRESS, CAMBRIDGE

ACKNOWLEDGMENTS

Ever since I first heard of him, some years ago, Alfred Bulltop Stormalong has seemed to me unique among the legendary figures of American folklore. There is something about him, hard to define, to be sure, which gives him a distinction all his own, although he belongs, quite truly, to a great fraternity. Like Paul Bunyan, Pecos Bill, and the others, Stormalong represents an indigenous tradition of bigness, of courageous imagination, of practical invention, and, indeed, of stubbornness. He is, in effect, the Yankee of the Yankees, a mythical figure created in their own image by a breed of men who have contributed an incalculable treasure to the greatness of the United States, the men and officers of the merchant marine, from the days of the China clipper to those of our own.

Unlike his brother heroes, however, Stormalong is something more than a purely native product. He is, as well, the Yankee in relation to the remainder of the world. Paul and Pecos Bill and Tony Beaver are fairly well confined in their exploits to the North American continent, with possibly an occasional excursion. They cover this territory extremely well. Stormy, however, carries the American flag into all the far corners of the earth, and with it the American spirit.

Not only does Stormalong bridge the oceans and carry the Yankee tradition far afield, geographically; he provides also a link between our young nation and the remote past. Many of the yarns which make up the cycle of Stormy legends are as old as civilization itself, and have been used over and over in the literatures of earlier nations, ever since the days of antiquity. The incident of the Stranger is obviously a variant of the biblical story of Jonah and the Whale. Stormy's fight with the Octopus could well be a modern version of the battle between Odysseus and the Old Man of the Sea. When Stormy "swallows the anchor," he places an oar on his shoulder and walks inland until the oar is mistaken for a threshing flail. Odysseus is enjoined by Teiresias of Thebes, in the Land of the Dead, to make

---

The Riverside Press
Cambridge · Massachusetts
Printed in the U.S.A.

iv

his final sacrifice to Poseidon at a spot so far inland that men know neither ships nor oars, "the wings of ships," and mistake his oar for a winnowing fan. The Kraken, of course, indulges himself in the same antics as does Charybdis. The Kraken also bears a certain family likeness to Grendel, the sea monster whom Beowulf slew.

One could go on for hours, but this is not the place for a dissertation upon the historical origins of the Stormalong legend. That in itself would occupy a series of volumes. Suffice it to say that Stormalong, the creation of the great days of American commercial development, is also a peculiarly American adaptation of the great lore of seafaring, in all waters and in all periods.

To Dell McCormick goes the full credit for envisaging a book about Stormalong. Other writers, including myself, have used certain elements and incidents from the many, many legends that surround the big sailor. No one else, however, has as yet pulled them together to make a whole volume about A. B. S. Mr. McCormick completed the research for his book, but was unable to finish a final draft before his tragically sudden death. Needless to say, it has been a privilege and a pleasure for me to take over the job where he had to leave it.

The sources from which Mr. McCormick drew his material fall into two categories. On the one hand, he consulted the previously published accounts of Stormy's history. These sources I think I know, since I have used them, too. They are acknowledged below. On the other hand, he learned many of the yarns which he added to the published literature from deep-water men. Neither Mrs. McCormick nor I know who these are. The best we can do to make acknowledgment to these contributors is to quote from a letter Dell McCormick wrote to the publisher:

> During the war I was an officer in the Army Transportation Corps, and as Troop Commander had many opportunities of talking with old-time sea captains, both in Alaskan waters and on the Atlantic run. Most of their stories about the mighty Stormalong followed the original pattern, but once in a while I would find an amusing new one. Over a period of years I was able to fill several notebooks on the strange and astounding adventures of old Captain Stormalong.
>
> The story of Algie the Sea Lion and the dreaded Giant Kraken were told to me by a Swedish harbor pilot. Many of the other tales such as Stormy's ride on the Grampus and the race with the Liverpool Packet were told to me by old timers on the cargo ships running between New York and Cardiff.

ACKNOWLEDGMENTS

Most of the old time seamen I talked to insisted Stormalong invented many of the refinements of modern navigation, such as weather reports and reefer ships . . . an old river pilot in Alaska assured me Captain Stormalong was the first to carry a cargo of frozen fish to the East Coast. It was mere child's play for him to fill the hold with fresh salmon and salt them down with ice chipped from icebergs. In many of the stories they called the ship the *Courser,* and others swore it was called the *Tuscarora.* It doesn't really matter. Everyone agreed there was never a ship to equal it in the old days.

For my own account, I should like to thank Mrs. Dell J. McCormick for her enthusiastic co-operation; Emilie Warren McLeod, for her assistance with certain technical aspects of preparing the manuscript, and:

Carl Carmer, for permission to use material adapted from a chapter entitled "How Old Stormalong Whitened the Cliffs of Dover" from his book *The Hurricane's Children,* copyright, 1937, by Mr. Carmer.

Coward McCann, Inc., for permission to adapt material from the chapter entitled "Captain Stormalong, the Revolution and Clipper Ships" from *Tall Tale America* by Walter Blair, copyright, 1944, by Coward McCann.

Doubleday and Company, Inc., for permission to adapt material from *Heroes, Outlaws, and Funny Fellows* by Olive Miller. Copyright, 1939, by Olive Beaupré Miller, reprinted by permission of Doubleday and Company, Inc.

Frank Shay, for permission to use material adapted from his book *Here's Audacity,* copyright, 1930, by him.

Anne Malcolmson

Contents

CHAPTER ONE

Stormalong

Goes to Sea

*C*APTAIN SNARD LOOKED UP
at the Blue Peter, the flag which proclaimed to the whole
of Boston Harbor that his ship, the *Silver Maid,* was ready
to leave for China. Her hold was filled with hides, beaver
skins, and good English coal. But everything was going
wrong! The cabin boy was at home, sick with the measles.
The shrouds and rigging lines were hopelessly tangled. The
anchor was stuck. Captain Snard paced the afterdeck,
fidgeting and looking at his watch.

His men tiptoed about their duties and whispered among
themselves. They knew enough not to cross the Old Man, as
they called him affectionately, when he was in a temper.
But they, too, knew that it was time to leave. The tide was
running out. Still, the Mate had not returned from town
with a new cabin boy. The lads in the rigging were getting
nowhere. And, strain as they might, the hands at the capstan
could not budge the anchor chain.

Suddenly from the dock the Mate's voice was heard, as he
ran to the ship. "Captain! Captain Snard!"

The Old Man leaned over the rail. "Have you got a cabin boy?" he shouted.

"No!" hollered the Mate. "There's not an experienced cabin boy to be had in Boston, sir."

"Then come aboard," roared the Captain. "From here to Canton *you'll* be my cabin boy!"

Neither the Mate nor the Captain had noticed a group of schoolboys sitting on the piles of the wharf beside the ship. Every Sunday the lads gathered on the docks to watch the ships sail, and to dream of the time when they, too, would be sailing. Among them was a youngster who had heard the Mate's call and the Captain's answer. This was his chance! He had always wanted to go to sea. The *Silver Maid* needed a cabin boy! With a light leap he cleared the wharf and landed on the starboard deck, right under the Captain's nose.

The vessel gave a lurch. Its topmast crosstrees brushed the roof of the warehouse on the pier. The *Silver Maid* listed dangerously to starboard.

"What is the meaning of this?" bellowed the Captain, who had had enough to irritate him already.

"Excuse me, sir," said the schoolboy, "I hear you need a cabin boy."

The Captain clung to the wheel to keep from slipping into the arms of the youngster who had jumped aboard. The latter was large for his age. He stood five fathoms, or about thirty feet tall; to judge from his appearance, he weighed several tons. No wonder the *Silver Maid* was listing!

"If you don't shift your weight more to the port side, I'll

need a salvage crew more than a cabin boy!" roared Captain Snard.

Stormy, the little fellow who was causing the trouble, blushed with embarrassment. "I'm sorry, sir," he stammered, and carefully placed one foot beside the port rail. The ship creaked and righted herself.

"Well!" said the Captain, wiping his brow and looking up at the lad. "What makes you think you can be a cabin boy?"

Tears came to the young boy's eyes. "The sea is in my blood, sir," he said simply. "All my life I've wanted to join the China trade."

"And how long is that?" The Captain meant to snap out his question, but the words came weakly.

"Thirteen years, sir," answered the little fellow politely.

"You're large for thirteen years," conceded the Captain, relaxing a bit. "Have you had any previous experience?"

"Oh, some, sir," Stormy replied, and proceeded to tell his story. The words tumbled out of his mouth as he spoke. His recital was full of gushes and pauses and "I-mean-sirs" and "You-see-sirs", which were perfectly natural in a boy of his age at an exciting moment.

Alfred Bulltop Stormalong, aged thirteen, was born in Kennebunkport, Maine, of a long line of seafarers. His mother's great-great-great-great-great-great-great-great-great-great-grandfather was the naval architect who designed Noah's Ark. His father's grand-grand-grand-grand-grand-granduncle sailed with Odysseus from Troy to the lands beyond the Cimmerian Seas. One of his ancestors, Leif Ericsson the Viking, was credited with the discovery of America long before Columbus, who, incidentally, was re-

lated to the family through a cousin on his mother's side.
Stormy's own father had been the first Yankee skipper, whom
Captain Snard himself had known, more by reputation than
personally.

Stormy really did have the sea in his blood. His veins and
arteries were filled with salt water, which shone out in the
bright sea blue of his eyes. He had cut his teeth on whalebone, and, in the days when he was too young to walk, he
had been cradled in a dory. On one occasion he gave his
mother fits when he tied his diaper to his teething rattle,
used it for a trysail, and headed out to sea while she was
preparing a formula of clam chowder for his evening bottle.
At the age of five he could handle any sailing vessel in the
Kennebunk estuary.

It was not until he started school, however, that he truly

learned to love the sea. Because of a shortage of primers, his teacher taught him to read from Bowditch's *Practical Navigator*. That set the course for his whole future life. Kennebunkport was a small town, and there were very few boys of his own age to play with. Stormy soon fell into the habit of swimming down to Gloucester or Provincetown, or sometimes Nantucket, after school to play. His mother knew he was perfectly safe and could handle himself in any sort of a squall. Her only objection was that the long swim increased his normally large appetite.

She did become angry, however, the fourth time he tried to stow away on a whaler at the age of eleven. Fortunately, from her point of view, Stormy was so large for his age (he had already reached a height of three and a half fathoms) that he was unable to hide himself successfully in a lifeboat. He was discovered before the whaler put to sea. As she told her friends later, she was cross because she worried that her son might be mistaken for a whale and cut up for oil and ambergris.

When the family moved to Boston, his mother knew that Stormy's days at home were numbered. She gave him her blessing, along with a note which he dutifully showed to Captain Snard, explaining that her son, Alfred Bulltop Stormalong, had her permission to join the crew of any vessel which would give him a berth.

The Captain was the father of seven daughters. Before Stormy had finished his tale, he had taken the boy to his heart. The Old Man, however, had to maintain discipline aboard his ship. He could not take on a new hand for whimsical reasons. The crew had gathered in a circle to hear the amazing tale of the young stranger. Therefore, Captain Snard felt forced to put the boy through a series of tests.

"Your background is fitting for a life on the sea, my lad," he said. "But I'll have to ask you a few questions to test your seamanship. What are the Horse Latitudes?"

Stormy's eyes shone at the chance to prove himself. "A belt of calms, sir, to be found thirty degrees north latitude, and another, thirty degrees south."

"What is the difference between a barque and a brigantine?"

"That is quite simple, sir," replied Stormy. "A barque is a three-masted vessel, with foremast and mainmast square-rigged, and mizzenmast fore-and-aft-rigged. A brigantine is a two-masted, square-rigged vessel which does not carry a square mainsail."

"Fair enough," said the Captain. "Now, can you recite the sails of the mainmast of the *Silver Maid*, from the bottom to the top . . . and with your eyes closed, of course!"

Stormy covered his eyes with his hands. "Main course, main lower topsail, main upper topsail, main lower topgallant, main upper topgallant, main royal, main . . . main . . . main . . ." Stormy paused and a wrinkle appeared in his forehead. He seemed to be stuck. A snicker ran through the crew. The Captain held his breath. Then Stormy's forehead cleared; he grinned from ear to ear. "Main skysail, sir! Of course, I knew it all the time!"

"Good boy," sighed the Captain, relieved that Stormy had passed the test. The Old Man stroked his chin for a moment. Then he held up a length of line for the little giant. "Show me what you can do with a piece of rope."

7

Stormy took the line between his fingertips, like a lady knotting a silken thread for her tapestry. He rubbed his thumb and ring finger together. Without further ado he held out his handiwork for the Captain to see. In the ten-foot length of cordage, Stormy had tied three perfect knots — a Bowline with a Bight, a Studding-sail Halyard Bend, and an Englishman's Tie!

"This is all very fine," agreed the Captain, trying not to show his enthusiasm for the boy. "However, theoretical knowledge is not enough at sea. You look to me as though you might be pretty clumsy. Do you think you can climb the rigging?"

"Aye, aye, sir!" Stormy was out of his jacket and halfway up the mainmast before the Captain could close his mouth. Up, up, up he went, hand over hand, until he was perched dangerously on the topmast crosstrees. His curly black hair, blown by the wind, fluttered out from the skysail yard like a shiny dark pennant. "Captain, oh, Captain, sir," he called down from his perch aloft. "It looks to me as though the lines are tangled. With your permission, sir, I'll straighten them out."

Captain Snard picked up his megaphone and shouted. "Be smart about it, son! And see that you don't make things worse!"

"Aye, aye, sir!" came the reply. From the deck the Old Man and his crew could see the little fellow reaching out to right and left, deftly unwinding the snarl of ropes which formed a spiderweb around him. One by one the lines fell into their proper places. Flushed with excitement, Stormy forgot himself. One last tangle remained at the port reach of the main royal yard. Without thinking, he hitched himself along the yard in order to get a better purchase on the line. Oooooops! Slowly, as his weight shifted, the *Silver Maid* heeled over to port. The gaping members of the crew skidded down the deck to the port rail. The Captain grabbed the binnacle to keep himself upright.

"Ahoy there! None of your tricks! Come down from that rigging before you ruin the ship," shouted the Old Man.

Stormy caught himself just in time. He scrambled back to the main mast. The ship righted herself. Phew! said Stormy to himself, That was a close one! Then, since he was an obedient boy, he grabbed a mainstay and zipped to the deck like a fireman down a brass pole.

Unfortunately, just as he started down, Porky the Cook emerged from the galley carrying a kettle of hot shark soup to cool on deck. As luck would have it, Porky and his chowder reached the exact spot at which Stormy landed at exactly the same moment. Cook, kettle, and Stormy disappeared behind a great splash of soup. The scalding, greasy liquid splattered the ship in all directions, ran over the decks and down the companionways and hatches. The crew, who had spent the morning polishing the deck and the brasses, roared in dismay. Porky was speechless with surprise and anger. Only Captain Snard, who was protected from the splash by the large wooden circle of the wheel, thought it was funny.

"That was a hot one!" he exclaimed to no one in particular. Then, struck by the wittiness of his own pun, he slapped his knee and felt very pleased with himself.

Stormy, of course, expected to be ordered off the ship.

The Captain, however, looked at him with indulgent affection as the lad apologized. "Boys will be boys!" was all he said. For no particular reason, the Old Man suddenly pictured his seven little daughters at home, properly working their samplers and learning their manners. What we need aboard this ship, he thought to himself, is a little liveliness.

The Captain would have hired Stormy then and there. The crew, however, were still angry about the soup. One further test was necessary to make them accept a new hand. A sailor needs knowledge and agility, but he also needs physical strength. It was obvious, looking at the boy, that he had strength, but it was difficult to know what kind of test would appease the disgruntled crew. The only thing the Old Man could think of was the stuck anchor. He had no hope that Stormalong could raise it, but the lad might be able to budge the chain. That at least was worth trying.

"Man the winches, lad," the Captain cried to Stormy.

"Aye, aye, sir!" Stormy answered to the Captain's order. The Captain watched solicitously as the boy pushed and strained against the capstan bar. Slowly, slowly, the heavy iron chain moved a little. There was a rumble as the anchor budged in its bed. Inch by inch, the chain clanked up around the capstan. Little by little, the stone which held the anchor gave way. Without warning, the resistance disappeared. Stormy, with one hand, turned the capstan. The anchor chain coiled up as though it had been woven of daisies.

A cheer went up from the crew. The men ran to the foredeck to watch the little giant wind the capstan. Without thinking, they burst into an old chantey:

"A Yankee ship comes down the river,
  Blow, boys, blow!
A Yankee ship and a Yankee skipper,
  Blow, my bully boys, blow!

"And how do you know she's a Yankee clipper?
  Blow, boys, blow!
Because her mast and yards shine like silver,
  Blow, my bully boys, blow!"

The *Silver Maid* strained and snapped her painters as the anchor lifted. Suddenly she was drifting out to sea with the tide.

"Unfurl the main course!" shouted the Bosun.

"Haul down the Blue Peter," shouted the Captain. "We're

off to Canton!" The men cheered as they raced to their posts. The *Silver Maid* put out to sea.

It was too late now for the Captain to dismiss the new cabin boy. He ordered the Mate to bring out the ship's ledger, and told Stormy to write down his name. Stormy, boy that he was, felt very grown-up. He had got the job he wanted and was finally a member of a ship's crew. Therefore he wrote himself down in the most grown-up way he could think of. Stormalong, A. B.!

Captain Snard took one look at the signature. "Stormalong, A. B.," he mused. "There's an able-bodied seaman for you," he commented to the Mate.

That is how Stormy got his first berth in the China trade. Ever since that day sailors in the merchant marine have written themselves down as Able-Bodied Seamen, with the initials, "A. B."

CHAPTER TWO

Boyish

Pranks

*N*OT LONG AFTER THE SIL-
ver Maid put out to sea, the Old Man knew that the new
boy was a rare find. Stormy's talents, indeed, were wasted
in a mere cabin boy. He made himself very useful on deck
in his off hours. Furthermore, his size was a menace below
deck. His head bumped the beams wherever he walked.
In his clumsy boyish way, he was forever knocking about,
breaking the glass in the portholes, splintering the walls of
the companionways. He caused Olaf the Big Norwegian,
the ship's carpenter, an unnecessary lot of repairs. Therefore, Captain Snard promoted the boy to apprentice seaman.

At Bridgetown in Barbados, a more suitable cabin boy was
signed on. Toby, the twelve-year-old orphan son of a
nephew of John Paul Jones, was a bright, winsome youngster.
He was as small for his age as Stormy was large. What Toby
lacked in size, he had in cleverness and friendliness. In no
time at all, he and Stormalong had become the best of
friends. The Captain was delighted to watch them playing

13

Hide-and-Seek together. More often than not, Toby hid in Stormy's jacket pocket.

Their real friendship began when the crew tried to play tricks on Toby. The lad had had no previous experience at sea. Smart as he was, he could not be expected to know all the ins-and-outs of a ship. Hammerhead Henderson the Sailmaker was not really a mean man, but he had been brought up the hard way. He came upon Toby sitting on a coil of line under the mizzenmast one late afternoon.

"Up with you, young feller!" he ordered. "The running lights need oil. It's your job to fill them. Get off your haunches and come back here with red oil for the port light and green oil for the starboard." Poor Toby! Nobody had told him this was part of his job. However, he was a willing worker. He searched the ship from stem to stern looking for oil for the running lights. There was plenty of oil on board, but none was red or green. In despair, Toby ran to Stormy to ask where the red and green oil was kept.

"Red and green oil?" asked Stormalong. "I never heard of such a thing."

Toby told him about Hammerhead's order. Stormy was angry. He knew that this was an old trick which the shellbacks liked to play on landlubbers. He explained to his younger friend that the running lights used perfectly plain oil. The red glass of the port lamp made it shine red, just as the green glass of the starboard light made it shine green. As he spoke he choked with indignation at the sailmaker who had played a dirty trick on a little kid. "I'll teach him a thing or two," he explained. "I'll make him tell you he's

sorry. Red and green oil, indeed!" Stormy moved off to give
the sailmaker a lesson.

"Wait a minute," called Toby, who was beginning to enjoy
the joke on himself. "Let's play a joke on him!" He whispered in Stormalong's ear. The two boys slapped their knees
and doubled over with laughter. Stormy ran to the hold
and brought back two barrels of plain, colorless oil. Toby
ran to the medicine chest in the Captain's cabin and brought
back a bottle of Mercurochrome and a bottle of oil of wintergreen. The medicines did their work.

"Well, I'll be a land-locked mud-turtle," laughed Hammerhead, when Toby presented him with two barrels of oil. One
was a ruby red, the other an emerald green.

Another time, Bullfinch the Bosun was battening down
the forward hatch when Toby asked him what he was doing.

The *Silver Maid* was running about two degrees north latitude at the moment and would cross the Equator shortly.

"We're about to cross the Equator, sonny," said Bullfinch
seriously. "That always gives the ship a bit of a bump. It
pays to have things battened down tight, because that ridge
is hard to get over. If I were you, I'd lash myself to the mast
until we've got beyond it. You never can tell what will happen." Bullfinch winked at Olaf, who was working nearby.
"You might give the boy a hand," he said. "You know how
it is when we cross the Line."

Olaf, an old-timer, was in on the joke. He showed a great
deal of concern for Toby's welfare, and obligingly lashed
him to the mainmast. Then the two shell-backs retired to
the foc's'le to laugh at their joke.

Stormy came by soon afterward, saw his friend tied to the
mast, and asked what was the matter. Toby urged him to
look out for himself. The ship was about to cross the bump
of the Equator.

"What bump?" asked Stormy. "The Equator's an imaginary line." He quoted Nathaniel Bowditch to prove his point.

"Oho!" laughed Toby. "They're playing tricks on me
again. Now, listen!" Stormy leaned over to hear what Toby
whispered into his ear.

Bullfinch and Olaf, who had finished their duties, settled
down in their hammocks in the foc's'le to laugh over their
joke. Every now and then they would look up the companionway to see little Toby tied to the mast, his hand over
his eyes, apparently searching for the ridge of the Equator
far out to sea. The two older men could hardly contain
themselves. The compass which Bullfinch kept under his

pillow showed that they must be right on the Line. The two of them hid their faces in their pillows to muffle their laughter.

Suddenly the *Silver Maid* trembled. Her beams shook and the two old sailors were hurled to the floor of the cabin. Bullfinch and Olaf looked at each other in horror! The ship must be passing over a volcanic sea. Perhaps a tidal wave had hit it. They rushed to the deck, to find Toby smiling innocently to himself — and just in time to see Stormalong's dark and dripping head emerge from the sea off the port bow. The Bosun knew immediately what had happened. Stormy, egged on by the little cabin boy, had jumped overboard, swum under the ship, and bumped the keel just as it crossed the Equator!

Captain Snard, who had watched the whole performance from the afterdeck, laughed until his blood pressure became dangerously high. He was still laughing when Olaf and Bullfinch carried him down to his bunk. The only satisfaction the two old sailors could get from him was the statement, "Oho! Oho! Oho! Boys will be boys!" And then he turned his face to the wall and laughed some more.

After several incidents of the sort, the older men grew to have respect for Toby and Stormy, and the teasing was stopped. Olaf and Bullfinch especially became fond of the lovable youngsters. Olaf even built a special bunk for Stormalong on top of the foc's'le, large enough for the boy to sleep in. It was a pretty sight on a starlit night to see him curled up like a kitten. From a special little pocket in his pillow, Toby's blond head could be seen resting against Stormy's black hair.

During a hot night in the Equatorial waters, well out of the Belt of Calms, Captain Snard noticed that the *Silver Maid* was running at half speed. She had a brisk wind behind her, her canvas was properly set, and he could not account for the heavy plodding of the ship. He sent the Mate forward to check the anchor.

The Mate had no need to look at the anchor. When he reached the forward deck, he could see what was wrong. Stormy was lying on his back in his bunk, with one foot over either side of the bow dragging in the water. No wonder the ship had lost speed. The Mate, who did not share the Old Man's tolerance of boyish carelessness, shook Stormalong and scolded him for his stupidity. Poor Stormy! He simply couldn't help causing trouble of one sort or another.

One calm night off Brazil Toby asked him to teach him to whistle. All the hands except those on watch were bedded down in the foc's'le. Stormy put his fingers to his lips and tried to whistle as softly as he could. Z-z-z-zing! Toby tried it, but no sound came out. Stormy put his fingers into his mouth again, this time forgetting to be quiet about it. Z-Z-Z-Z-ing!

Bullfinch the Bosun, a light sleeper, woke as though he had been shot. He turned in his hammock and listened intently. The shrill piping sound came again. Z-Z-Z-Zing! Z-Z-Z-Zing! It meant but one thing to Bullfinch. The wind was rising and ripping through the rigging. He blew his whistle and roared to his boys to man their posts against a rising gale. You can imagine their surprise to stumble on deck and find the sea as calm as glass. There was no wind at all.

Z-Z-Z-Zing! There it was again!

19

This time Bullfinch knew what it was. He winked at the hands and pointed to Stormy, who had not noticed the commotion and was patiently whistling for Toby.

"Cut out that racket!" called Bullfinch. "Can't you let a man sleep?"

From then on Stormalong was self-conscious and tried his best to keep from causing difficulty. There were times, however, when he couldn't help himself. For instance, one night he and Toby were talking quietly before they went to sleep. Stormy was in the middle of a description of his early school days in Kennebunkport when his voice suddenly broke. The sentence had started in his usual childish soprano, but ended in a deep bass. Once again Bullfinch was awakened, this time with the notion that the *Silver Maid* had run into a fog bank and was blowing her horns. He listened carefully before getting out of bed. The deep, double-bass tones continued over his head. Then he heard words, and made out the question, "Did you ever read Bowditch's *Practical Navigator*?" Bullfinch relaxed and went back to sleep. He knew that it was only Stormy again.

The only member of the crew who was not easily won over to an affection for Stormalong was Porky the Cook. Adolphus Don Sebastian Whittier Green, the tyrant of the galley, was a temperamental man who had little patience. So far as he was concerned, teen-age boys were a nuisance. He resented the extra work that was forced on him by adolescent appetites. Also he could not forget the day when Stormy had landed in his soup kettle.

Porky was an important person aboard the ship. He was charged with the personal welfare of the crew. He looked after their aches and pains as well as their hunger. As ship's doctor, he kept a shelf of medicine bottles in his galley. These were labeled to show what ailments they were meant to cure. EYE. EAR. NOSE. THROAT. STOMACH-ACHE. Each of the bottles contained a dark brown bitter fluid. Without the labels, it was impossible to tell them apart. As a matter of fact, they were all the same prescription. Porky had shopped around Boston before the ship sailed. Being a frugal Yankee, he bought his supply from a provisioner who offered him a barrel of medicine at half price. He divided it up among the big jars. He was quite pleased with himself, because now none of his boys could claim any better treatment than any other. They all got the same.

Porky thought of himself as Dr. Green, ship's surgeon. He had, however, a greater mission to fulfill as ship's cook. His greatest achievement was his Barnacle Pie. Like any other chef, he refused to give away the recipe for his masterpiece. The general consensus was that the pie was based on a cornmeal crust with a variable filling. Toward the outward end of a voyage, the crust became tougher and harder to chew, while Olaf's sawdust pile grew smaller. The men figured that the ratio of sawdust to cornmeal in Porky's pie-crust could be determined by the distance from the home port.

As for the stuffing, in good days it was made of beef from the harness casks on the after deck. In the fishing grounds it might contain such delicacies as codfish tongues, shark livers, and dolphin fillets. In hard times, anything could happen. Even boots, Nor'westers, rusty harpoons, and Sunday clothes might make their appearance from under the crust. If a seaman lost his earring or his pet parrot, he didn't bother to look for it. Sooner or later, it would turn up in the pie.

Stormy tried his best to make friends with Porky. At last he found the proper way. He had captured a baby sea-lion, a cuddly little thing with spotted silky fur. Except for its shape and its whiskers, it might have been mistaken for a dappled faun. Knowing that Porky loved animals, Stormy gave the pet to the cook. Porky was delighted. He named the baby sea-lion Algernon and called him Algie for short. Everywhere the cook went, Algie would follow. The boys, Stormy and Toby, made a little white cook's hat just like Porky's for the new pet. This touched Porky to the heart.

You know how sea-lions are, friendly and intelligent, but essentially lazy. Petted as he was by his new master, Algie grew fatter and fatter and lazier and lazier. He loved to cuddle beside the stove in the galley where it was warm. Porky gave him tidbits and let him lick the pots and pans. One of his best tricks was to stir the stuffing for the Barnacle Pie with his flipper. It amused everyone on board to watch the sea-lion, a cook's hat on his head, holding a big pan in one flipper and stirring the batter with the other. Even Captain Snard stopped in the galley occasionally to watch Algie, who loved attention, could hardly be persuaded to stop stirring when it was time to put the pie in the oven.

As time went on, Algie grew so fat that he took up most of the room in the galley. He couldn't squeeze through the galley door to go up on deck. Porky had to move out the pantry shelves and the chopping block to make room for him. At last the time came when Porky had to have the stove turned around to face the galley porthole, so that he ould stand outside to cook. There wasn't enough room inside even for him.

There is no telling what might have happened if the Mate hadn't lost his temper. At the end of a cold watch on a foggy night, he went to the galley for a cup of coffee. It was black dark. All he could make out in the gloom was a white cook's hat in the galley door. He thought, of course, that it was Porky and ordered a cup of coffee.

"Oick! Oick!" cried Algie, who was glad to have company.

"No conversation, please," snapped the Mate, who was tired and in a bad humor. "Just coffee, and be quick about it."

Algie couldn't understand English. Porky had always talked to him in baby-talk. Consequently, he thought the Mate wanted to play.

"Oick! Oick! Oick! Oick!" Algie gurgled and reached out to give the Mate an affectionate kiss. A cold wet snout and a bristling set of whiskers nuzzled the Mate's cheek.

"Get that blubbering sea-going tramp out of here!" the Mate bellowed in fury. The crew came running just in time to see him reach for the big meat cleaver on the wall above Algie's head. "I'll teach you to do tricks to me," he was shouting, "I'll cut you up into little pieces and stuff you into the next Barnacle Pie that softheaded animal-trainer of a cook mixes up for us."

Porky had reached the scene by this time. White with fear and anger, he threw his arms around his darling pet, who, by this time, was shrieking with terror. Bullfinch grabbed the Mate's arm and tried to take away the cleaver. Captain Snard heard the uproar from the afterdeck and

came to investigate. He felt sorry for Porky, but he agreed
with the Mate that Algie must *go*. He was too much for
the ship and things could only get worse! The only
solution seemed to be to kill the creature, so that he could
be cut up and removed from the galley in sections. Poor
Porky fainted when he heard the sentence! He loved Algie
more than he had loved anything in all his life. But the
Captain's word was law on the ship.

Stormalong felt almost as bad as Porky when he heard the
Captain's order. He had a great affection for the sea-lion
who, like himself, was too large for his age. Tears came to
his eyes. Suddenly he thought of a plan that might save the
situation. He begged the Captain to let him try.

"I think I can do it, sir," Stormy pleaded. "I'll try not to
cause too much damage." The Captain thought for a moment, then he nodded.

"Go ahead, son," he agreed.. "It won't hurt to try."

Stormy reached into the galley and placed his hands under
Algie's flippers. He braced his feet against the foremast and
the mainmast. He pulled as gently and powerfully as he
could. There was a straining and a creaking as Algie's fat
stomach stuck in the galley doorframe. Poor Algie screamed
with pain! This was what Stormy had counted on. As Algie
screamed, his stomach muscles contracted. Stormy gave an
extra tug. Algie was yanked free. He flew up over every
one's head and shot out to sea, like a cork popping out of a
bottle. Stormy himself almost fell overboard from the force
of the tug.

Not much damage was done. The doorframe was buckled
but Olaf was able to fix it. The Mate was pacified, once the

sea-lion had been got rid of. Porky, of course, was terribly saddened by the loss of his pet. However, he was grateful to Stormy for having saved Algie's life. For some days the sea-lion followed the ship, his white cook's hat still on his head. Porky spent his off hours at the stern rail, tossing bits of Algie's favorite dishes overboard.

The time came, of course, when Algie left them. The *Silver Maid* passed a small island on whose shores were basking a herd of sea-lions. The sight of one of their own kind in a strange white head-piece caught the fancy of the youngsters in the herd. They waved their flippers and "oicked" loudly to catch his attention. They succeeded. Algie, fickle as he was, turned off to join them. With the aid of the Captain's binoculars, Porky caught his last glimpse of his pet, happily playing tag with his new playmates in the waters off a rocky Pacific island.

CHAPTER THREE

Stormy Tries Whaling

SOME OF THE MOST EN
joyable evenings aboard the *Silver Maid* were spent on the
forward deck when the crew gathered to mend their clothes
One night the talk turned to whaling. Several of the men
had sailed aboard spouters, as whaling ships were known
and had great stories to tell. An argument broke out be
tween Olaf and Hammerhead as to whether or not the story
of Jonah were true. Hammerhead claimed that no whale
he'd ever heard of could swallow a man. Right whales
everyone knew, had a curtain of whalebone at the back of
the jaw through which they strained their food. Even the
great sperm whale had a throat no bigger than a man's fist

Olaf contended that the story came from the Bible, and
therefore it must be true. Furthermore, he pointed out, all
of them knew cases of men who were actually Jonahs — men
whose presence aboard a ship was a jinx.

Suddenly, to everyone's surprise, the Stranger joined the
conversation. The Stranger was a wizened little sailor who
kept entirely to himself throughout the voyage. He had

signed on in Boston, but after months at sea none of the crew knew anything about him. He was a good seaman, however, and the men respected his obvious desire to keep his own counsel. Toby and Stormy had thought him a rather mysterious fellow, and for some reason, were a little afraid of him. Now at last he was speaking quite freely and companionably.

According to his story, the Stranger had spent twelve years on a spouter, following the whale from the Bering Sea to the Falkland Islands. On one trip aboard the *Maid o' Gloucester* they were after the sperm whale, when a big bull was sighted. "Thar she blows!" shouted the look-out. The boats were lowered, and the chase began.

There was a young feller in the lead boat, the best artist with a harpoon on the seven oceans. His iron dug into the big bull's neck; the boatsmen braced themselves for a wild Nantucket sleigh-ride. The whale, however, fooled them. He turned quickly, and one flip of his giant flukes splintered the whaling boat and sent the men flying into the sea. The other boats raced to the rescue as the whale swam away. All but one of the men were found, all but the young feller who had thrown the harpoon. For hours they searched the water, hoping to find at least a trace of him. But not a sign, not even his hat, showed on the surface. He had simply disappeared.

It soon became obvious that he was gone for good, and the boats returned to the spouter to take up the business of whaling once more. Several days later they spotted the big bull. This time he was captured after a great struggle. His huge carcass was made fast beside the *Maid o' Gloucester*, and the cutters went to work, removing layer after layer of the precious blubber. When they reached the whale's stomach they realized something was very odd. A great bulge protruded from one side of it. Furthermore, the bulge shifted and squirmed faintly as though something were moving inside.

With great care they slit an opening in the big belly and reached in. Out came the limp arm of a man. Silently the cutters laid the skin open. There inside, more dead than alive, was the young feller, the harpoonist. His arms and legs moved feebly, his eyes stared into space, he mumbled to himself strangely, and did not recognize his shipmates as they gently lifted him out and carried him to his bunk.

For days on end, in spite of their tender care, the young feller remained delirious. When at last he recovered, he refused to talk about his adventure. No one could pry a word out of him. In other respects he seemed to be all right. The only marks left by the experience were his silence and the fact that the tattooing on his chest and back had turned a brilliant emerald green from the whale's gastric juices.

The Stranger lasped into his usual silence at the end of the story. Several of the men tried to draw him out about what happened to the young feller after that, but he shrugged as much as to say he did not know.

Some weeks later, when most of the crew were resting below, Toby ran tiptoeing to Stormy and motioned him to follow quietly. He stopped against the wall of the foredeck house, and pointed to the foc's'le. There stood the Stranger alone, stripped to the waist, washing his shirt in a bucket. All they could see was his back on which was tattooed a whaling ship in full sail. The tattooing was as green as sea-weed in the sun.

After the incident of the Stranger, Stormy had a period of sleepless nights. At first he thought his trouble was simply growing-pains. He could not even discuss the matter with Toby. When he did sleep, he dreamt of great adventures in the open seas, following a great white sperm whale. At last it dawned upon him what was wrong. He loved the sea and the men aboard the *Silver Maid,* but to a young lad thirsting for adventure the life was too tame. After all, the China trade was a little monotonous — the same old cargo, the same old routes, the same old ports! The only excitement came when the ship struck a storm. In the hands of a skill-ful skipper like Captain Snard, even storms were not very dangerous. In a spouter, though, you never knew where you were going. For three years, a whaling ship could follow the fancy of the great beasts it was after. The North and South Poles were common ports of call. Something inside Stormalong, some growing desire to try his luck on a spouter, tickled and teased him.

At last he confided in the Captain and asked his advice. Captain Snard smiled sadly at the lad. He recalled only too well his youthful days when he, also, longed for adven-ture above all. He hated to lose the boy, but perhaps it was just as well for Stormalong to get this tormenting urge out of his system while he was still young. The Old Man spoke gently as he pointed out the disadvantages of whaling. This had its own monotony. There were months on end when no whales were sighted, the crews whittled whalebone into scrimshaw work to keep from going mad with boredom.

Whalers were dirty and smelly; the food was poor; life was hard. The Old Man could see that his words were making very little impression on the imaginative boy.

When the *Silver Maid* reached Boston, Stormalong, with the Captain's blessing, left her. The *Gridiron*, a whaler out of New Bedford, was provisioning in the harbor, and Captain Snard introduced his young protégé to her master, Captain Speedicutt. With a mist in his eye, Snard grasped Stormy's hand and made him promise that if he ever returned to the China trade he would look up his first master before anyone else.

* * * * *

Life aboard a whaler suited the young giant exactly. There was much to learn. Even though no whales were sighted for the first few months, Stormalong was kept busy. He listened to the conversation of the crew, plied them with questions, until, in his own mind, he felt that he could handle any job on the ship. For days on end he practiced throwing a harpoon, until he was as skillful as any man on board. He could throw his cap over the rail, let it float for fifty fathoms, and then spear it with his iron as neatly as though he were playing a game of darts.

The day finally came when the wished-for call, "Thar she blows!" rang down from the look-out. Stormalong's heart raced. This was his first chance to spear a "critter." Off to starboard, a school of grampus were romping in the sunlit water. In his excitement, Stormy forgot himself completely. He grabbed his harpoon, took aim, and let fly even before the men could lower the whaleboats into the water. The iron struck home into the back of a young bull. The grampus leaped and twisted, but Stormy pulled with all his strength. Little by little the line shortened, until the twenty-foot grampus was flipped aboard the *Gridiron* to the deck at Stormy's feet.

The men, who had watched this performance in amazement, suddenly burst out laughing! They had been stunned at the display of the young giant's strength, but now they were tickled at his ignorance. This was not the way to handle a whale, even a little one like a grampus.

"Now, what are you going to do with it?" the Mate yelled at Stormy.

Stormalong blushed. He realized too late that his impulse had run away with him. He had been told how to handle a whale and should have known better. The thing to do was to haul the creature alongside the ship so that the cutters could reach it and go to work. The ship was fitted with gear for the purpose, but the gear was over the side, not on the deck. *What* was he going to do now?

Stormy thought wistfully of his little friend Toby, back on the *Silver Maid*, whose cleverness had always found an answer to a difficult situation. He tried to imagine what Toby would suggest. He could think of only one thing, which wasn't very clever at that. It was, however, the only thing to do. With a grunt, he picked up the big slimy fish in his arms and dumped it over the rail. The men lashed it to the side, and the cutters got to work. For weeks the men laughed themselves to sleep over the picture of Stormy with the grampus at his feet on the deck. Fortunately, he was good-humored, and learned to laugh at the episode himself.

Perhaps because of this incident, Stormalong applied himself anew to his trade and soon learned all of its tricks. He learned, too, to control his tendency to forget himself. In time he became famous among whalers all over the North Atlantic, who heard rumors of the boy's extraordinary success. He gradually learned to harpoon a whole school of whale at once, but this required careful timing and teamwork with his fellow crewmen. When a herd was sighted, the whaling boats were lowered, and each boat's crew took its station. The harpoons were handed up to Stormy, who stood on the forward deck. He placed the irons carefully between his fingers. He could manage four at once. When the Bosun blew his whistle, Stormy hurled his javelins, the boatsmen leaned on their oars, and the four whaling boats leaped out to follow their prey. It was like the start of a sculling race. Stormy's aim was infallible. Four whales at a time! It became necessary for the ship's cooper to arrange four sets of gear for the cutters to work from. The *Gridiron* was the envy of every captain from the North Pole to the South.

Word got around among the whales themselves, too! By early winter, there was not a right whale or a bowhead or even a porpoise to be found in the Atlantic grounds. They had all retired to the North Pole, to hide under the ice-cap from the terror of the seas. The tough little *Gridiron* followed in happy pursuit. Captain Speedicutt was too pleased with his success to think of the dangers involved. As an inevitable result, the *Gridiron* got stuck in the ice. The men tried everything. Stormy, who felt responsible for the predicament, offered to pull the ship free. Try as he might, even he could not budge the vessel which was caught fast in ice ten fathoms thick. There was nothing to do but to wait for spring.

There was plenty of food on board. The ship was sturdy and not likely to be crushed. The only danger was boredom. The crew soon found a pastime to occupy them. Not far from the ship was an Eskimo village, where, it was said, lived a number of pretty Eskimo girls. The sailors decided to go courting. They cleaned themselves up in the icy water of melted snow, shaved off their beards, and put on their Sunday clothes. One by one and two by two they slid over the side of the *Gridiron* and made their way to the little huddle of igloos. One by one and two by two they returned to the ship dejected. The girls would have nothing to do with them. Stormy alone had not made the trip.

Not without some malice, the rest of the crew urged Stormy to go to try his luck. He didn't want to do it at all. In the first place, he was by now only seventeen, and while he was a man in strength and skill, he was still an inexperienced boy. He had known very few girls in his life, and always felt like a fool in front of them. The teasing of his mates, however, began to get under his skin, and at last Stormy determined to take their dares. He wished that Toby were here to tell him what to do.

Good old Toby! Why, of course! Stormy suddenly remembered a big box of salt-water taffy that Toby had given him as a parting gift when he left the *Silver Maid*. Girls liked candy.

To say the least, the members of the crew were surprised when Stormy returned to the *Gridiron*. He was as pleased

JOSHUA TOLFORD

as punch with himself. Perched on his big shoulders and his folded arms sat twelve young Eskimo girls, squealing and giggling and flirting, and all munching salt-water taffy. He set the young ladies down on the deck. The Mate pulled his flute out of his pocket, and the cook got out his bull-fiddle. When the sailors recovered from their shock, the dancing started. It was the gayest party ever held in that part of the world. Stormy, who didn't know how to dance, watched from the sidelines. When the party was over, he carried the guests back to their homes. The next day the ice cracked, much to Stormy's relief. He had enjoyed showing the crew that he could make a hit with the girls, but the prospect of being stuck in an ice-floe with twelve flirtatious young Eskimos was more than he could face.

As the ice-cap cracked and split up into icebergs, the whales lost the shelter which the winter had afforded them. They were forced into the open ocean, to the infinite pleasıre of Captain Speedicutt and the men aboard the *Gridiron*. Throughout the spring of the year, the ship followed the fleeing herds, picking up the choicest specimens almost without an effort. Before they had left New Bedford, the Captain's friends had offered the usual toast to a departing whaler, "To a greasy voyage!" There was no doubt that this trip was the greasiest on record. The ship's holds bulged with barrels of whale oil. The decks were slippery from the constant cutting and rendering.

Success, however, can be dull. Stormalong's accurate aim and the teamwork which developed between him and his mates made the business of whaling routine. Even ambitious Captain Speedicutt had to admit that there wasn't much zest in the life any more. What the men needed was some excitement. The opportunity soon presented itself.

Not far from the Azores, the home grounds of the great sperm whale, the look-out sighted what appeared to him to be a huge uncharted island of white marble with a tall mountain rising to the sky. There was much speculation as to what it could be. For a while it was thought that this might be the lost island of Atlantis, which, according to the ancient Greeks, had disappeared from the Western Seas in an earthquake. Captain Speedicutt himself climbed into the crow's-nest with his binoculars to have a good look. Just as he did so, the great fountain disappeared. After a long minute, it reappeared in an enormous feather of white spray. This was no island. This was a huge white whale, spouting and basking in the sunlight.

Stormalong with all the brashness of youth was anxious to go right after the creature. The Captain, however, was less enthusiastic. A whale as large as this one, at least a hundred fathoms long, presented a number of practical problems. Even if they should succeed in killing the beast, the ship's gear was not large enough to handle him. There was not enough room to accommodate the mountains of blubber and the oceans of whale oil which he would produce.

Stormy, who, by this time, had learned to use his imagination by figuring out what Toby would think of, had an answer for the Captain's doubts. He suggested that once the whale was dead, the ship tow it into the New Bedford dry-dock, where gear could be set up to take care of the necessary work. The refinery was nearby, and the whole job of cutting, rendering, and refining could be done quite simply. His suggestion made a good deal of sense. The Captain, who was never one to shrink from a chance to add to his laurels, was won over without much urging. It was agreed that the *Gridiron* would make one last attempt at glory before she turned back to her home port.

The preparations were made carefully, while the ship bore down on the basking whale. Stormy took his stand on the foredeck with his heaviest harpoon in hand. The men stood tense with excitement beside the whaleboats, ready to lower when the word was given.

The whale, unfortunately, was as clever as he was large. Long before the *Gridiron* had sighted him, he had sighted the ship. This was an old story to him. How many spouters he had sent to Davy Jones's locker he couldn't remember. He had long since worked out his own technique for handling situations of the sort.

Just as the *Gridiron* came within striking distance, he

took one lazy look around, spouted insolently, and dove into the depths of the ocean. Far away on the horizon he re-appeared, and a white feather of spray rose into the air, as much as to say, Come and get me, if you dare!

His arrogance made Stormy and his mates angry. Once again the *Gridiron* gave chase. This, of course, was what the whale expected. He chuckled to himself as the ship came closer and closer. Lazily he rolled in the sea and eyed his approaching antagonists. There was something about this spouter he didn't like. The size of the young feller standing on the foredeck with a harpoon irritated him. What was the world coming to when the human race grew specimens almost as large as whales? This young man would have to be taught a lesson that would make him go back to land and stay there.

As the *Gridiron* approached, once more the whale dove into the ocean. But this time he appeared right under the bow of the ship and flipped the keel with his giant flukes. Whaleboats, men, barrels of oil were sent flying into the air. Only Stormy stood his ground and managed to hurl his harpoon at the beast. The iron barely grazed the whale's back, but enough to sting and hurt his pride. In fury he turned quickly before Stormalong could seize another iron, and spat right in the harpoonist's eye. Then he disappeared.

This was too much for Stormy. To miss his strike was bad enough, but to suffer the humiliation of having a whale spit in his eye was worse. He turned crimson with rage, raised his clenched fist in the direction of the retreating whale, and muttered, "I'll get you, you varmint of the sea!"

His chance came the next day. The great whale, confident

that he had frightened his pursuers off the ocean, was resting
from his exertions. Now Stormalong had the advantage
The *Gridiron* approached the beast from the back. The
sperm whale, of course, can see only to the front and the
sides.

Stormalong had melted down all the ship's irons into
one enormous harpoon. He had sharpened the point until it
was as keen as the Captain's razor. He took careful aim and
let it fly. This time it sank into the whale's back. The startled
bull leaped and twisted so suddenly that Stormalong lost his
balance. He held on to the line, but his feet slipped from
under him and he was pulled from the deck into the water.

And now began the greatest Nantucket sleigh-ride in all
history. The whale dove to the ocean floor, twisted and
turned and rose to the surface in spirals and fancy figures
trying to shake Stormy loose. Stormy held tight. The whole
Atlantic churned with the beast's efforts to free himself. But
Stormy held tight. Southward they flew like the wind, some
times brushing the coast of North Africa, sometimes the
coast of Brazil. At last the whale headed into the Straits of
Magellan, where he hoped to break Stormalong's grip against
the sharp rocks. Stormy saw what was coming and saved
himself in time. With an extra effort he climbed hand over
hand up the line until he sat astride the whale's back.

Out into the Pacific they shot, with Stormy perched on the
beast's neck, like a cowboy on a bronco. At thirty knots
the white giant shot across the ocean in a westerly
direction, blinded with fury. Stormy could see what the
whale could not. In the far distance on the horizon loomed a
low black mass. Land! Stormalong figured it might be the

coast of China, but he wasn't sure. He shut his eyes as the
whale hit the beach at full speed. They were going so fast
that they cleared the shore and landed in a field two miles
inland.

The force of the landing knocked both Stormalong and the
whale unconscious. Stormy was so exhausted from his wild
ride that he slept for two days. When he awoke, he was
surrounded by strange people, jabbering a strange tongue
and poking curiously at him and at the carcass of the big
white creature beside him. He was too dazed at first to
realize that these were indeed Chinese villagers and that he
had landed unceremoniously in a small town not far from
Canton.

In a sense he was safe at last. On the other hand, he was
alone in a foreign country, with no money and no friends.
If Toby were only here to tell him what to do!

The thought of Toby reminded him that the boys had
learned a little pidgin English on one of the *Silver Maid's*
early trips. They had also met Chinese before, when they
put into Canton, and knew that these were the most curious
people on earth. Immediately Stormalong saw the solution
to his problem. He found a villager who could speak pidgin
English and enlisted his help. The whale, by now, was dead.
With the villager's assistance, Stormalong built a fence
around the great beast. He had his new friend paint a sign
in Chinese characters which announced, "The Largest Min-
now in the World! Admission, Two Yen!"

Word of the new wonder to be seen spread quickly
throughout China. Young and old, babies and grandmothers,
peasants and mandarins, all came to see the sight. In no

time, Stormy was rich. He had more than enough money to hire a palanquin to take him to Canton, so he gave a share of the whale show to his new Chinese friend and took his departure.

In Canton, Stormalong felt shabby beside the beautifully robed Chinese and the smart-looking ship's officers in the uniforms of all nations. His clothes had suffered from his wild ride on the sea. There were no tailors who could outfit him in the Western fashion, so Stormy bought himself a mandarin coat of rich black silk. Across the back in Chinese characters not unlike the pattern of a dragon, his initials A. B. S. were embroidered in gold thread. He even had his hair braided into a long black pigtail.

Suitably clothed, Stormalong strolled down to the waterfront to see what ships had come in. A new clipper, the *Lady of the Sea* out of Boston, was tied up beside the wharf loading tea. She was a fine ship, and Stormalong suddenly felt homesick for the happy days aboard the *Silver Maid*. He looked over her lines from bowsprit to poop rail. Suddenly a familiar and beloved head appeared in the porthole of the master's cabin. It was Captain Snard.

The Old Man was puzzled at the giant Chinese mandarin who stood beside the mainmast and called him by name. The more he looked, the more he realized that there was something familiar about the stranger. In spite of the Chinese robe and the black pigtail, this was no Oriental. The eyes were as blue as the ocean itself.

"Don't you remember me, sir?" asked the stranger politely.

The Old Man rubbed his eyes. He could hardly believe it, but without a doubt this was his young friend Stormalong.

"Welcome aboard, my boy!" he shouted. He wrung Stormy's big hand as best he could. "Where have you been? And how did you get into that rig?"

Stormy, of course, told the Captain the whole story of his career as a whaler. Their talk lasted far into the night. The more he talked and the more he listened to the kindly old man, the more Stormy knew that he was homesick for the China trade. Whaling was fine in its way, but this was the life for him. Before dawn, he had signed on as the Bosun of the *Lady of the Sea*. Captain Snard himself brought out the big ship's book and showed Stormy where to write his name, "Stormalong, A. B.," just as he had written it seven years before.

CHAPTER FOUR

The Fight with the Octopus

STORMY WAS DELIGHTED to be aboard a merchant ship again. He had had his fill of adventure for the time being and whaling had lost its glamour. For one thing, a tea packet is a clean ship. For another, now that he had the responsible position of bosun, life was not dull.

He felt completely at home as soon as he set foot on the deck of the *Lady of the Sea*. His joy was tripled when he discovered a number of old friends aboard — Bullfinch the Bosun, who was now the Mate, Olaf the Big Norwegian, Hammerhead Henderson, and Porky the Cook. These had all followed Captain Snard when he took over his new command. Only Toby was missing from the crew of the *Silver Maid*. Bullfinch told Stormalong what had happened to the cabin boy.

Toby stayed with the ship for one voyage after Stormy left her. It was plain to everyone, however, that the little lad was lonely without his big playmate. The sailors did their best to keep him cheerful, but they were grown men. He needed a companion of his own age. He was too small in

43

HAMMERHEAD
HENDERSON   CAPT. SNARD   BULLFINCH   PORKY   BIG OLAF

size, furthermore, ever to be more than a cabin boy. He could not furl a topsail to save himself. He weighed too little to be able to hold down a corner of canvas. A slight gust of wind was enough to send him flapping into the air. It was plain that he had no future on the sea.

Clever as he was, he made up his mind to seek his future on the land. With a slight inheritance from his father's family, he set himself up as a ship's provisioner in Boston. When the ship had last left that port, he was doing nicely. Even the sharpest Yankees in the town had to admit that the young man from Barbados was a smart trader and likely to prosper.

Captain Snard was delighted to have Stormalong aboard his ship once more. He took a fatherly pride in the manner in which the boy had developed. No longer the awkward, self-conscious lad of thirteen who had first caught the Old Man's fancy, Stormy was now an assured young man of twenty, poised, skillful, and resourceful. His shipmates respected him, not only for his gigantic size and physical strength, but for the fairness and firmness of his decisions. In short, he was growing up to be a real leader among men.

Two days out of Canton harbor, the *Lady of the Sea* ran into trouble. In those days, the waters of Southern China were infested with pirates, evil creatures who lurked in the bays and inlets of the coast to prey on merchant vessels. The shipping lanes offered many a rich prize coming to and from

44

the Indies, laden with tea and silks and jewels. The *Lady of the Sea* was no exception.

Suddenly out of nowhere, four black Chinese junks raced across the water toward the *Lady*, two across her bow, two closing in from the stern. The look-out shouted to the new bosun, who was taking his turn at the wheel.

"Pirates!" he cried.

The crew shivered when they heard the dreaded word. In Canton they had listened to stories of the barbaric cruelty of the Oriental pirates. Compared to these, Blackbeard and Henry Morgan were gentlemen, who were content to let their victims merely walk the plank. These Chinese buccaneers, however, were specialists in the art of torture and refined brutality.

Stormalong alone among the crew did not seem to be alarmed as the junks bore down upon the merchantmen. He conferred with Captain Snard and Bullfinch, and then took full charge.

The *Lady of the Sea* still carried under the forward hatch a shipment of molasses bound for Australia. Stormy ordered the big barrels hoisted up to the deck. He told the men to stave in their sides. The thick, sweet, sticky syrup oozed out from the gashes in the wood onto the decks. Then, at his command, the crew of the *Lady* climbed the rigging.

The pirates, seeing the sailors shinnying up the masts of the Yankee packet, thought the latter were frightened and would surrender easily. With horrible yells of joy, the brigands rammed their junks alongside the *Lady*, lashed the ships together, and swarmed over the rails, brandishing great carved swords. This was indeed an easy prize!

To their dismay, however, their feet skidded and slipped and slithered in a sticky ointment. They fell on top of each other and were as helpless as flies on flypaper.

Stormalong waited until the last pirate had boarded his ship, a grizzled, ugly old fellow with one eye and a toothless grin, whose dress identified him as the captain of the marauders. Stormy reached out for a coil of rope, quickly knotted a loop in the end, and swung it over the old pirate's head as neatly as a painter over a pile. He jerked the rope tight, and the pirate chief hung helplessly in mid-air from the crosstrees, kicking and screaming, his arms pinned to his sides.

Bullfinch and Olaf were prepared to follow Stormy's example. Then the other men of the crew caught on. In a moment, ropes were flying and snapping through the air. One by one, the brigands were strung up from the yards of the *Lady of the Sea*, where they squirmed and swung uncomfortably in the wind.

Captain Snard agreed with Stormalong that the freebooters should be brought to justice. Therefore, the *Lady of the Sea* altered her course, and returned to the mainland, towing the four junks, and carrying their ugly crews in her brig. At Hong Kong, their prisoners were turned over to the authorities for trial by the courts of admiralty. Stormalong politely declined any personal reward for their capture. Instead he asked permission to take a few of the younger pirates back to the United States. These were boys who were not really bad at heart, but had been forced into a life of crime by their wicked elders. Stormalong was sure that properly educated they could become useful citizens.

His wish, of course, was granted. Four young Chinese pirates were allowed to return aboard the *Lady of the Sea* as stewards and galley boys, under Porky's special care. The idea was a good one. Out of gratitude for their deliverance, they taught Porky how to make such dishes as chow mein and bird's-nest soup, which provided a welcome change in the menu when the Barnacle Pie became monotonous. They studied their lessons diligently. By the time the ship reached Cape Horn, the four young Chinese could recite the Declaration of Independence in a singsong unison. When at last the ship reached Boston, their unfortunate early life had long since been forgotten. They left the sea, and established themselves as peaceful citizens in their new home, where they founded the first Chinese restaurants and hand laundries.

* * * * *

The *Lady of the Sea* did not reach her home port without another adventure, however. Off the Island of Guadaloupe in the West Indies, she was forced to anchor in a little cove to ride out a hurricane. The storm raged throughout the night, but no great damage was done. The men slept peacefully in their hammocks, confident that Captain Snard, Bullfinch, and Stormalong had taken all the necessary precautions.

The morning found the sea as smooth as green glass. It was safe for the ship to continue her voyage. The Old Man ordered the hands to man their posts for sailing. The crew at the capstan strained against the bar to raise the anchor. It started to move smoothly, and then stopped.

"Blow, boys, blow," the men sang as they pushed harder still against the capstan bar. The anchor gave a little, rose a foot or two, and then refused to move any further. In fact, the chain unwound a fathom or two, as though the anchor itself were being pulled back to the bottom of the sea. They tried once more, and the same thing happened again.

Bullfinch reported the matter to Captain Snard on the afterdeck. Stormalong overheard the Mate's report. "I'll have a try at the capstan, sir," he told the Captain, and went forward to add his great strength to that of the men.

Not even Stormy could budge the capstan when the anchor settled back to the ocean bed. The water was clear, but the harbor so deep that it was impossible to see what was holding the heavy iron at the bottom. The assumption was that the chain must be fouled in a coral reef.

"Well," said Stormalong, "there's nothing to do but to have a look." With that, he peeled off his jacket, unlaced his boots, and dove over the side. Down, down, down he went until he disappeared in the dark green gloom below. The Captain and the men crowded the rail to watch his descent. They all knew that Stormalong was a powerful swimmer and that he could stay under water for a long time. The seconds, however, passed into minutes; the minutes ticked themselves off; and still no black head appeared from below.

While they waited anxiously, the water began to heave. Waves appeared around the ship in the otherwise calm water of the bay, and spread out in circles until they broke against the shore. The *Lady of the Sea* began to pitch and toss, although the wind had not risen at all. Then through the water could be heard a muffled shrieking and roaring.

Streaks of black liquid spurted up through the froth of the churning waters below.

The Old Man and Bullfinch held on to the lifeboat davits and leaned far over the side, hoping to make out what was happening. The dreadful thrashing of the waters and the rocking of the *Lady of the Sea* made this too dangerous. They were terrified for Stormalong, thinking that an earthquake was cracking the ocean floor or perhaps an undersea volcano was erupting. They were completely unable to help him in any way.

At last the terrible roaring and the lashing stopped. The sea calmed itself a little, but the waters were so muddied from the disturbance that nothing could be seen. Then came a series of strange, short upheavals. The waters would churn, the black liquid streaks would shoot out in all directions, and the noise would resume. Then silence. Each time the uproar was shorter, and the silence longer.

Bullfinch and the Captain looked at each other in bewilderment. This could not be an earthquake or a volcano. The only explanation either could think of was that Stormalong was fighting a terrible battle with some demon of the sea. The longer and longer silences were ominous. Neither man dared to say what each thought. Stormy must be weakening.

A final churning was followed by complete calm. Nothing more was heard. Slowly the ruffled waters smoothed themselves; slowly they cleared. But still no sign of Stormalong. Every man aboard the *Lady of the Sea* hung far out over the rail trying to catch a glimpse of the beloved bosun.

When ten minutes had passed without a sound, the Old Man turned his head away, blew his nose, and slowly trudged up the companionway to the afterdeck house. Bullfinch removed his cap, and with tears in his eyes, followed the Captain. The two men stood quietly, afraid to look at each other for fear they would break down. Stormalong was lost. There was no doubt of it.

Then a commotion began on the port side of the forward deck where the four young galley boys had posted themselves. Their piping voices, squealing in Chinese, could not be understood, — but obviously something was happening. Olaf noticed also that the capstan bar was moving in slow, regular jerks, as though something were tugging at the anchor chain. Then a cheer rang out from the men who had rushed to the port rail.

Slowly, wearily, as though the effort cost all his strength, Stormy pulled himself up hand over hand on the anchor chain. His shirt had been torn from his back. His trousers were ripped and ragged. His body was streaked with bruises and smears that seemed to be black blood. Bullfinch and Olaf lowered lifeboats and tried to help him as his head broke through the surface. Stormalong, however, shook his head and waved them aside. With one final effort, he pulled himself over the rail and collapsed panting on the deck. He had only enough strength to motion to the men to pull up the anchor chain.

Captain Snard bent over the young man's dripping head. "What was it, son?" he asked gently. "Can you tell me what happened?"

Stormalong opened his eyes enough to see the Old Man's worried face. "Giant octopus, sir," was all he could murmur. He fell into a deep sleep.

Giant octopus! The mere thought of it sent a chill down the Captain's spine. These deadly beasts, great black creatures with long tentacles, lurked on the floor of the sea, picking up any living creatures which they fancied for food in their slimy black arms. Each of these arms was studded with suction cups which could paralyse whatever came their way. No man was a match for the villainous devilfish. The men who heard Stormy's whisper were struck dumb with horror. Stormy had leaped into the water without so much as a knife in his belt to defend himself.

Captain Snard put his coat over the sleeping bosun and waved to the gaping seamen to do the same. Then, to cover his emotion, he snapped at the capstan crew. "Get along! Hurry up! Raise the anchor!"

The big winch responded immediately to the men's pushing. They chanted the song, "Blow, boys, blow," under their breath, lest they awaken Stormalong. Slowly and heavily the anchor chain was wound around the capstan.

"Look here, Captain," shouted Porky, pointing excitedly over the side as the big iron approached the surface. Lashed to the anchor by its own tentacles was a giant octopus. Its body measured nineteen feet across, and its arms were thirty feet long. The beast was indeed a terrifying sight. Helpless as he was, it was no trouble at all for the crew to finish off the big devilfish. Octopus steak became a regular ingredient of the Barnacle Pie for the remainder of the voyage.

As soon as Stormalong awoke from his heavy sleep, the Old Man and the crew plied him with questions about his battle. He was too modest to boast about the exploit, or even to enjoy talking about it. He finally admitted, however, that it had been something of a fight.

"When I got to the bottom," he told his audience, "that old giant squid was sitting there with four of his arms holding onto the ocean floor, and four to the anchor.

JOSHUA TOLFORD

" 'Begging your pardon, sir,' I says to him, 'I'd appreciate it if you'd let go of that anchor. The *Lady of the Sea* is ready to sail for her home port.'

"The squid pretends he doesn't hear me, and looks the other way. I taps one of his arms to get his attention.

" 'I haven't time to bandy words about,' I says to him, 'My men are anxious to get home.'

"At that he looks up and yawns and taps his mouth with one of his arms and drums the tips of four other arms against the ocean bed, as much as to say, Possession is nine points of the law, and what are you aiming to do about it?

"His attitude made me see red. I grabbed one of the arms he had wrapped around the anchor, in the name of Peabody, Adams, and Webster, the owners of the *Lady of the Sea*. With my fingers I pried the suckers loose. That got his steam up, and for a moment I thought I was a goner. We wrestled a bit, and I realized that I could manage only one tentacle at a time. That old devilfish, however, had one idea in his mind. He was *not* going to give up that anchor. This stubborn notion cost him the battle, because it kept four of his arms occupied, two on the anchor and two on the rocks. When I figured this out it wasn't so bad. I could grab the tip of a tentacle and stretch it, so that I was just out of range of the others. From there on in, I just held on until he stopped fussing and caught his breath. Then I tied up the tentacle in a Double Carrick Bend and started on the next one."

Stormalong looked thoughtful for a moment. "You know, the octopus is a mighty animal. And a stubborn one."

CHAPTER FIVE

Stormalong Swallows the Anchor

WHEN BULLFINCH LEFT the *Lady of the Sea* to become master of his own ship, it was only logical that Stormalong should take his place as first mate. Stormy was young for such a responsible position. Everyone agreed, however, that he deserved it.

Captain Snard, who was growing older, was overjoyed to have his trusted assistance at the wheel of the ship.

Stormy himself was thoroughly happy for a time. He enjoyed having the afterdeck to himself. Here he would stand for hours on end, managing the great wheel with a flick of his little finger, daydreaming of the great things he would achieve in the future. Some day he would have a ship of his own, large enough to do him justice. The best naval architects in Boston would design her. He could see her in his mind's eye, as long as an island, as swift as a hurricane, and as enduring as the pyramids of Egypt. Whenever he dreamed of her, he was likely to be a little careless and to shift his weight suddenly. The *Lady of the Sea* lurched and he had to come back to reality to right her.

Meanwhile, the figure of Stormalong standing on the afterdeck, his shoulders level with the main royal, became familiar along all the shipping lanes. The *Lady* no longer had to identify herself when she passed another ship. For the first few months, other seamen, seeing her profile against the horizon, thought she had some new sort of rigging — an extra mainmast square-rigged in the stern. They soon realized that what they thought was a royal course on the stern mast was simply Stormalong's square shoulders.

In time, however, Stormalong knew that something was wrong with him. The first symptom was an unnatural hunger. He had an enormous appetite, which Porky worked day and night to satisfy. The little cook saw to it that the big mate had all he asked for — a dozen ostrich eggs sunnyside-up for breakfast, a dory full of clam chowder or shark soup for lunch, a side of beef or a steak cut from a great sperm whale for dinner — with occasional barrels of coffee between meals. Stormalong appreciated the cook's effort. He realized that the ship had a limited space for food, and that the men of the crew had to be fed, too. He wished to be fair to everyone. Therefore, when a fresh Barnacle Pie was baked in one of the unused lifeboats, he ate only half of it

MISTER STORMALONG, MATE

and left the remainder for the men. He could have eaten it all. More often than not, he left the table hungry and pulled his belt a little tighter.

As a growing boy, he had thought very little about his appetite. Boys are always hungry. Stormy assumed that he was just a natural boy. But now that he had reached young manhood and had stopped growing, the gnawing hunger worried him. He no longer dreamed about the great ship he would command one day. More often than not, he dreamed about food — about dinners consisting of a schooner of soup for an appetizer, a herd of cattle medium rare, and a small volcano of chocolate ice cream with a river of marshmallow sauce. He grew thin and pale. He almost convinced himself that he was starving to death, or that possibly he had a tapeworm.

The next symptom was restlessness. Stormalong could not sleep. Olaf had built for him a large bunk behind the wheel, but even so he had to curl his great length in order to fit into it. In the mornings, his knees and elbows ached, his muscles were stiff. He wanted to toss and turn all night, but this, of course, he could not do for fear of upsetting the ship. Consequently, he lay looking at the stars and worrying, night after night. Black circles appeared under his eyes. He kept his troubles to himself, but Captain Snard noticed the signs of ill health and was secretly anxious about the young man.

Then Stormy realized that he was very lonely. He longed for Toby, whose humor and cleverness had kept him amused in their early days together. The Captain was his good friend; they had many interesting conversations, but the Captain now liked to do all the talking. Furthermore, Captain Snard had seven marriageable daughters on his hands. He had lately got the habit of telling his mate how pretty Abigail was, how clever Patience was, how demure Lucy was, and so on, until he frightened the junior officer into a week of sleepless nights. While he loved the Captain as he loved his father, Stormy was tempted to jump ship.

There was no one else to talk to satisfactorily. Olaf and Hammerhead and Porky and the others were his friends but none of them was a man of his own stature. Their bodies were much smaller than his. Similarly, their imaginations were more limited.

Stormalong now began to suffer from nightmares. He would awake from his cramped half sleep to think himself bound like Gulliver, while little men the size of ants scrambled up his sides and paraded on his chest. Usually the nightmare ended when a little bride, named Patience or Abigail or Lucy, was led up to his chin, a tiny little trumpet like the sound of a mosquito squeaked through the air, and a miniature Captain Snard shouted, "I now pronounce you

JOSHUA TOLFORD

my beloved son-in-law." The icy sweat which formed on Stormalong's forehead as he awoke dripped down from the afterdeck to the main deck.

Night after night he lay on his back awake, afraid to go to sleep for fear he would dream, looking at the tops of the tall masts and the wide reach of the horizon. All of a sudden, he knew what he must do! The masts had once been tall trees in a great forest. The forests were said to grow beside the wide prairies, where a man could put his foot down without fear of upsetting a ship. That should be the life for him!

In the morning he spoke to the Captain. As soon as the ship docked in Boston, Stormy picked up an oar from a lifeboat and lifted it to his shoulders.

"Mates," he said in his farewell speech, "I'm going to walk inland. As soon as a stranger who's never seen or heard of the sea or anything to do with it asks me what this oar is, I'm going to settle down. I'll know I've gone far enough to get the salt out of my mouth and the rocking of the sea out of my sleep!"

*   *   *   *   *

JOSHUA TOLFORD

And so he did! On and on Stormalong plodded, the oar on his shoulder, past the Berkshires, past the Hudson River, along the Erie Canal to the Great Lakes. He walked through woods and fields, but somehow he kept to the waterways. He met river-men and canal-men and lake-men — but they all recognized his oar for what it was. Finally he struck out into the forests of the Northwest Territory. At last he met the stranger he had been waiting for.

"Howdy," said the stranger. "What's that there threshing flail doing over your shoulder?"

Stormalong tipped his cap, but did not understand completely. "What's what doing?" he asked as politely as possible.

"That there threshing flail," answered the stranger. "There won't be an acre of grain around here to thresh until the woods is cleared and the fields is planted. What you need is an axe and a plow, brother!"

Alfred Bulltop Stormalong, the terror of the North Atlantic Seas, felt his oar. The stranger thought it was something with which to thresh grain! This was what he had longed for. With an impulsive gesture, he hugged the newcomer.

"Hold on, there," yelled the stranger. "Be careful, son! Friendship is friendship and all that, but on the frontier a man can't be too cautious. Now set me down, and I'll give you some advice, since you seem unaccustomed to the country!"

Stormalong set the little man down gently, and listened to what he had to say. Here was land, all a man could ask for, almost for the asking. All he had to do was to stake out a claim, file an application with the Government, clear the

trees and stumps, plow the ground, plant the seed, build
himself a house, and settle down for life.

"Thanks, Pop!" said Stormy, when the older man had
finished. "I'm sure proud to have met you. I'll do as you
say!"

And with that Stormalong did as he was told. He didn't
bother sawing down the trees. He simply pulled them up
by the roots, and broke off the branches. With his old scrimshaw knife he cut the trunks up into clapboards for his new
cabin. He had more lumber than he could possibly use, so
he traded a small carload of it for an old plow. With this
he plowed his acres. Not for him a team of horses to pull the
plow! He just pushed it through the earth by his own brute
strength. By the end of summer he was settled. His cabin
an oversized replica of Captain Snard's cabin on the *Lady
of the Sea,* was as tidy a little home as a man could wish for

Stormy worked hard at his farm. Just as he had mastered
all the tricks of navigation and of whaling, he soon learned
all the tricks of farming. He listened patiently to his neighbors and learned what he could from their talk. At the end
of a year he was the most prosperous farmer in the whole
frontier community.

When a drought hit the section, the potato crop for mile
around was lost. The vines withered and turned brown, the
potatoes shriveled and died. But not Stormy's! Stormalong
worked day in and day out trying to save his crop. He
worked so hard that the sweat poured from his arms and hi
back in a little river which watered the plants. Being a
generous man, when his own plants had been saved, he
worked over the plants of his neighbors, and saved these

oo. When at last the potatoes were harvested for market, hey proved to be the tastiest spuds in the world. No extra easoning was necessary when they were mashed. Their alty flavor could be traced to the sweat of Stormy's brow.

In time, many legends grew up about the giant and his arm. Many of the lazier farmers refused to admit that his uccess was due to his own hard work. They claimed that ie had magic powers, and invented stories to prove their point. Anyone who knew the man, knew that the yarns were ntirely out of character.

For instance, it was said that Stormalong planted ten-penny nails and grew a crop of crowbars. This was obvious nonsense. It was claimed also that he planted horsehairs, and produced a harvest of Morgan colts. This, too, was idiculous. Stormalong had practically no interest in horses. He had no need for them to pull his plow. He was much oo large to ride comfortably in the saddle. Horses were just a nuisance, so far as he was concerned, always getting underfoot, and unable to do anything which he could not do better alone. The silliest story of all was spread by a ealous orchardman in the next county, who declared that Stormalong planted copper pennies in the dark of the moon and reaped bank notes and dollar bills. In spite of the petty malice of these gossips, Alfred Bulltop Stormalong was re-pected by his fellows. He was admired for his great strength and his diligence, and loved for his generosity and gentleness.

There were certain aspects of farming in which he could never succeed. For a time he kept chickens, but he had to give them up. They were too tiny for him to handle. He had to gather the eggs with a pair of tweezers. His fingers were too large to pick them out of the nests naturally. Once, when he was running to help a neighbor whose barn had caught fire, he stepped on a chicken-house in his haste, as a smaller man might step on ant-hill. That was the end of his interest in poultry.

Dairy farming also was difficult for him. He bought a fine herd of Guernseys and set them out in the south pasture. He loved to watch their sleek fawn-and-white bodies against the soft green of the hillside. But he was clumsy at milking. The whole herd produced hardly enough milk for his own supper. The time spent in caring for the beasts could be spent more profitably in the fields. So he sold the cattle, and traded his wheat and corn for milk and butter.

Failure of any kind discouraged him. Even though any-one could see that cows and chickens were not suited to his

JOSHUA TOLFORD

alents in the first place, Stormy was depressed at having to give them up.

One factor which made him conscious of a feeling of oneliness was the matter of speech. Try as he might to learn and talk, Stormalong still thought in the language of the ea. There were many New Englanders in his neighborhood, but these came from the inland counties of Maine and New Hampshire and Vermont. They did not really understand his salt-water expressions.

When a seed salesman came to his farm to ask directions o the next settlement, Stormy replied, "Keep a straight ourse until you come to the red barn off the port bow. Then swing over on the starboard tack and head north-northwest. It ain't more than fifty fathoms on from the road ork."

The salesman did not recognize Stormy's speech as English. He had heard that many immigrants from the North ountries of Europe had lately moved in to the Territories. He wished to be friendly, and held out his hand.

"Welcome to the United States of America, the Land of Opportunity," he said!

This declaration flabbergasted Stormy. He was too surprised even to object when the salesman turned left at the oad fork. Any fool should have known that a starboard tack meant a right turn!

On another occasion, Stormalong was visiting a neighbor when a storm cloud suddenly appeared in the western sky. The farmer's wife was in the back yard hanging up the laundry. Wishing to be helpful, Stormy warned her politely:

"There's a squall coming, ma'am. Better reef them stuns'ls

afore she hits. She'll rip 'em right off the rigging." Having
explained the coming storm to his satisfaction, Stormalong
himself began to take down the sheets. The poor farm
woman thought he was trying to steal her linens and shouted
to her husband for help.

One of Stormy's most generous gestures had an unfortunate effect. He appreciated all the helpful advice which
had been given him when he started farming. When the
county courthouse was built, he wanted to show his appre-
ciation. He sent to Boston for a fine clock to mount in the
courthouse tower. It was a beautiful clock in a teakwood
case and struck the hours on a ship's bell of clear brass. At
last it was installed. The grateful citizens honored Stormy
in speeches that lasted all day.

The trouble was that the clock was made for ship's time.
At four in the afternoon it struck eight bells. At five in the
morning it struck two bells. Naturally, the farmhand
thought it meant two o'clock and turned over and went back
to sleep, instead of getting up. The cows weren't milked
on time. The hens weren't fed. No one knew what the hour
was except at eight o'clock. It nearly drove the countryside
crazy trying to figure out what time it was.

At last the clock had to be taken down. This hurt Stormalong more than he would admit; it convinced him that he
would never be really at home away from the sea. The more
he thought about it, the sadder and more restless he grew.
Whenever he pushed his plow, his muscles ached, remind-
ing him that a sailor's life is all pulling, not pushing. Whenever he ate a supper of potato soup, he longed for some
of Porky's clam chowder. He hadn't seen a clam or an oyster

or so long he could hardly remember what one tasted like.
The more he looked around his acres from his front porch
on a summer evening, the more the horizon looked the same.
It was a pretty view, but the fact was that Stormalong was
bored with it. No sails on the horizon! No shore in the distance! Nothing but fields and trees that were there day after
day after day.

Before his discontent had driven him to leave the farm,
a tornado ripped across the countryside. A tornado, as
everyone knows, is one of the most terrifying storms of the
central plains region of America. Its black funnel-shaped
cloud reaches to the earth and travels across the land at
terrific speed, destroying everything in its path. The other
farmers rushed to their cellars for safety, but not Stormalong.
Something in the air reminded him of the great hurricanes
through which he had ridden on the ocean. He climbed to
the roof of his barn to keep his eye on things.

When the full force of the storm struck, it carried everything with it, including the barn. Instinctively, Stormalong
knew what to do. He rigged a sail, fore-and-aft, with an
old tarpaulin which he used to cover his corn crib. Without a wheel or a compass, he kept the sailing building under
control. Around and around they sailed, over hills and
forests and towns, riding out the crazy course of the storm.
At last the force of the wind abated, and the barn came
down — right in the middle of Lake Michigan.

Suddenly Stormalong felt perfectly at home. He was on
water with a sailing vessel of a sort under him. The thought
of turning back to his farm was more than he could face.
He stopped for a moment and took his bearings. The wind

67

had died to a steady westerly breeze. The temptation was too much for him. He trimmed his sail for the voyage before him, headed up to the Straits of Mackinac, down through Lake Huron, and on to the East. Nothing stopped him, until he passed through the Cabot Straits into the open Atlantic Ocean off the coasts of Newfoundland and Nova Scotia. The wide calm bosom of the sea welcomed him home. And Alfred Bulltop Stormalong knew that he would never again make the mistake of "swallowing the anchor."

It was not long before a passing ship noticed the strange craft. A red barn with a corn-crib cover for a sail was unusual in the fishing grounds of the Grand Banks. A trawler out of Boston was the first ship to come and investigate. Her captain was cautious as he edged her into position to take a look at what might be some newfangled craft. He raised his glass to take a good look. As soon as he spotted the thick black hair and the sea-blue eyes of the giant navigator, he relaxed. The captain, like all other mariners, recognized the great Stormalong when he saw him. He had heard the sad story of Stormy's deserting the sea. When he realized that the strange craft was a barn, he guessed what had happened. Stormalong had deserted the land and was returning to his proper trade.

The captain of the trawler bowed and took off his cap as he shouted through his megaphone, "It will be my privilege, sir, to offer you a berth to Boston!"

CHAPTER SIX

A Capital Ship

*W*HEN ALFRED BULLTOP Stormalong reached Boston aboard the fishing trawler, he knew that he was at home. He forgot his years of farming, and the discontent that once had made him leave the sea. The sight of a harbor full of ships made his heart beat faster. He felt the salt water pounding in his veins.

News of his return spread quickly through the city and throughout all New England. From Stonington to Eastport, sailors heard the words, "He's back!"

No one asked who "he" was! Everyone knew. Singly, in pairs, and in whole crews, officers and men left their stations and hurried to Boston to welcome the great man. At first the shipowners didn't know what to make of their ships riding empty in the ports. They assumed that a strike must be going on. They were about to send a message to the Governor of Massachusetts to ask him to put the striking seamen in irons, when they learned what had happened. Stormalong had come back! The shipowners followed their sailors to Boston to greet the fabulous mariner.

What a party there was then! All the cooks of Easter
Massachusetts turned out to prepare the celebration unde
Porky's direction. Nothing was too good for Stormalon
At first there was talk of setting up a long table on T wha
for the feast. This seemed impractical, so T wharf itself be
came the table. The guests sat in skiffs and dories around i
edges.

In spite of the hundreds of persons who gathered for th
occasion, it looked as though much of the food would b
wasted. The guests stuffed themselves. When the speeche
began, nevertheless, there were still bowls of chowder an
barrels of lobster and shucked oysters waiting to be eate
While the speakers were having their fun, Stormalong sa
at the head of the wharf, idly nibbling at the leftovers. By th
time the evening's entertainment was finished, he had cleane
up all that remained. It was the first time, he said to hin
self, that he had ever had enough to eat.

After the official ceremony was done, Stormalong's ol

riends gathered around him. They sat talking together for
wo weeks, hearing what he had to say about life on his farm,
nd telling him all the news of the shipping world. Toby,
vho had become very prosperous and was now a shipowner
imself, knew the gossip of the ports. Bullfinch and Ham-
ierhead and Olaf, who had become captains, knew the
ossip of the seas.

The only person missing from the party was Captain
nard. Stormalong grieved when he heard why. The Old
Ian had died of a broken heart when his favorite first mate
ift the sea. He had been given a fine funeral, his body
iwered to Davy Jones' locker from the side of the *Lady
f the Sea.*

Stormy was considerably relieved to learn that six of
aptain Snard's daughters had been married, and the
ieventh, little Patience, was about to become the bride of
is friend Toby. When he heard this, he knew it was per-
ictly safe for him to visit the family in Quincy to express
is sorrow at the death of his beloved former master and his
iy at the approaching felicity of his old shipmate.

One subject of conversation cropped up during the party,
ut was dropped as soon as it was started. Apparently a new
iip was a-building somewhere on the New England coast.
ormalong could overhear only bits of sentences about it,
ut it aroused his curiosity. A young cabin boy happened
i be bragging to his friends that he had seen the wonder,
ist as Stormy passed the group of youngsters.

"She's so big," the lad was saying, "that . . . that . . . well
. . that you can't see the bow from the stern without a tel-
icope!"

The big sailor turned around quickly. He laid his little
finger lightly on the boy's shoulder.

"What's this you're talking about, son?"

The poor cabin boy froze with fear. His teeth chattered
as he realized that he was being addressed by Stormalong
himself.

"N-n-n-nothing, sir," he stuttered, shrinking from the
giant's curious gaze. Before Stormalong could repeat his

JOSHUA TOLFORD

question, Olaf appeared as if by magic and cuffed the lad.

"That'll teach you young whippersnappers to mind your own business!" he shouted to the boy, who disappeared as fast as his heels would carry him. Then, blushing, the Big Norwegian turned to Stormy. "Little pitchers have big ears — and big imaginations!" was all he would say.

Stormy was completely puzzled. This sort of behavior was not at all like Olaf. He decided to ask Toby.

Toby met his question with a look of blank innocence. "I haven't any idea what you're talking about," he replied. "Come, friend, you're feverish with excitement." But Toby, too, blushed as he spoke, and Stormy noticed that he had his fingers crossed.

Stormy could see that he would learn nothing from his old companions. He determined that he would find out for himself as soon as he returned from his visit to Captain Snard's family. He did not have long to wait.

One fine morning he was sitting on the sea-wall, gazing at the smooth green swell of the water, when a misty object began to take shape on the far horizon. He had heard tales of mirages seen by men lost in the desert. This vision shifted and sparkled before his eyes, just as an image of an oasis might sparkle before a thirsty wanderer in the desert. This image, however, was a ship. An immense ship, which seemed as long as the arm of Cape Cod itself. The more he looked, the less imaginary it appeared. He could see several mainmasts, and a whole forest of foremasts and mizzenmasts.

As he strained to make out more details, a schooner, as large as the *Silver Maid*, was lowered from the side of the apparition and made its way into the harbor. Stormalong could soon see that she, at least, was real. He knew then that the vision on the horizon must be real, too. He dove off the sea-wall and swam with all his might for the horizon.

You can imagine his surprise when he pulled himself up beside the great white vessel. Standing at the deckrail was a committee of shipowners in their Sunday clothes. Toby, the chairman, was the first to speak.

"Welcome aboard the *Tuscarora, Captain* Stormalong," he cried, bowing from the waist. His eyes twinkled. The other members of the committee followed his example.

"Welcome aboard, Captain Stormalong," they repeated, even though some of them were choking with merriment.

Stormy shook the water from his eyes and stared at the unexpected vision of twelve gentlemen in frock coats, bowing and grinning. His first reaction was that this was one of Toby's pranks.

"Look here," he turned sharply to his old companion. "It's bad enough, when you return after a long absence, to know that your friends are keeping something from you. It's bad enough to have to swim Massachusetts Bay to find out what they're lying about! But it's *too much* to be made the butt of their jokes at the end of the swim!"

Toby sensed immediately that Stormalong was quick to feel hurt. He clambered up a mainmast until he could whisper in Stormalong's ear. "This is not a joke, as you put it. It's a surprise. It's a present for you. These men have built this ship out of respect for you! This is *your* ship!"

Stormalong was very modest. He was overcome at Toby's statement. He was also embarrassed at this expression of affection for himself and at his cross misinterpretation. He now understood Olaf's angry hushing of the little cabin boy and Toby's crossed fingers. Even the most hard-bitten of the Yankee merchants was moved to see the tears in Stormy's eyes.

Toby was the first to recover himself enough to lead the conversation. He explained to his friend that the ship had been designed originally to tempt Stormy back to the sea.

New England shipping had not been the same since he "swallowed the anchor." She was almost completed when Stormy had come back of his own accord. Therefore the builders decided to present her as a real surprise! It had been very difficult to keep the secret.

He then led the party to the Captain's cabin. On the door was a plate with the name, "Captain Alfred Bulltop Stormalong," engraved in gold. Inside was a bunk five fathoms long, carved with scenes from Stormy's adventures aboard the *Silver Maid,* the *Gridiron,* and the *Lady of the Sea.* A life-size portrait of Captain Snard hung beside the little shaving mirror above the washstand. Every detail was planned for Stormy's comfort.

"You'll have to excuse me, gentlemen," Stormalong gasped. "I don't know what to say."

Toby, however, broke the tension. He opened the medicine cabinet and pointed proudly to two barrels on the upper shelf. On their labels in big letters were printed "Port Oil" and "Starboard Oil," and under these in fine print, "Mercurochrome" and "Oil of Wintergreen." At this reminder of an old prank, Stormy began to laugh. He regained his composure and the ice was broken.

The *Tuscarora,* as the giant ship was named, was indeed as fabulous as her captain. She was so large that her lifeboats had to have lifeboats. It was impossible to see the top of her great mainmasts except on a clear day. The little cabin boy was right. One needed a telescope to see her bow from her stern. Some notion of her size can be gained from the story which the owners told Captain Stormalong of the difficulties they had while building her.

A thousand square miles of North American forest were cut down to provide the planking for the *Tuscarora's* decks and the ribs for her hull. Fourteen ships, even so, had to be despatched to Sumatra and the Malay Peninsula to procure teak wood for her cabins and interior trim.

The sails posed a problem. Three hundred and twenty sailmakers from England and New England gathered to cut and hem the canvas. Unfortunately, New England is a hilly region. No spot could be found flat enough to stretch the main course. For a time it seemed as though the project would have to be given up, until someone remembered the Sahara Desert. Canvas, sailmakers, and all were shipped to Africa and set to work on the great flat waste.

Altogether, it took three years to build the *Tuscarora*, and she was still not completely finished in all details. When the skeleton ship was finished and she was ready for launching, a national holiday was declared. The President of the United States, the Cabinet, the Congress, the Governors of the Eastern States, the Presidents of the Chambers of Commerce, the entire shipping industry, the whole population of New England, and one or two Ambassadors from countries interested in trade came to the launching. Unfortunately, while the President was making his speech, and before his wife had a chance to swing the bottle of champagne with which she was to christen the ship, the *Tuscarora* broke loose from her moorings and slid down the ways. She hit the water with a splash that caused a tidal wave as high as the Customs House Tower.

Miraculously, none of the spectators was injured or drowned. The only loss was the President's tall silk hat, which was recovered several days later by a British merchantman in the Gulf Stream off the coast of Ireland.

Stormalong, of course, was interested in all that the owners had to tell him of the *Tuscarora's* history. He was even more impatient, however, for a chance to try her out. He had his opportunity when the owners asked his advice about certain details which wanted finishing.

Stormy could see that several things needed to be done. The trouble was that neither he nor anyone else had ever sailed a ship of this size. It was impossible to foresee all the problems which might arise. He suggested a trial run before any more work should be undertaken. All the essential elements needed for sailing were ready. With a skeleton crew, he proposed to make a test cruise, and, at the end of it, present his suggestions. This was a very sensible proposal. The owners were delighted.

    ❈   ❈   ❈   ❈   ❈

With a mere handful of men and officers, five hundred in all, Captain Stormalong made a quick trip around the world in his new ship the *Tuscarora*. He was happier than he had ever imagined it possible to be. At last he had a vessel in which he could move around without fear that a shift of his weight would turn her keel over. The sixteen-foot wheel of Philippine mahogany fitted his hands as a wheel should fit the hands of a steersman. He no longer had to touch a spoke delicately with his little finger.

Stormalong had been troubled in his other berths on the sea by some vague discontent or other, but not aboard the *Tuscarora*. He could have sailed forever, simply enjoying himself and relishing the thrill of the great ship's response to his direction. He had **work** to do, however. He had promised a full report on her behavior and on possible ways of improving it. By the time the ship returned to her home anchorage outside the tip of Cape Cod, his report was ready.

There is no point in setting down a copy of the report here. It was full of technical matters, most of which are of interest to naval architects only. There were a number of suggestions, however, which can give you some idea of how remarkable the *Tuscarora* was and how well Stormalong understood the problems she created.

The most serious difficulty presented by her size seemed at first too basic to be overcome. When Stormalong ordered all hands aloft to reef the upper sails, it took his men two and sometimes three days to get up and back. If he sent them up on Tuesday, they came back on Thursday. Fortunately, the weather was pleasant throughout the trial run, but this might have been serious in a stormy season. The masts had been of California redwood trees, two thousand

JOSHUA TOLFORD

years old, as broad at the base as a small building. Stormalong had been much impressed at a visit to New York by a new invention called the dumb-waiter, which could be hauled up and down a shaft of rope between a basement kitchen and an upstairs dining-room. It saved many steps.

Why not hollow out the masts and fit them out with dumb-waiters? he asked himself. This suggestion was put into his report and duly adopted. The dumb-waiters, or elevators, cut the time for the men to climb aloft. They did not solve the whole problem. It still took too long for the men to reach the ends of the yardarms.

Stormalong had a hunch that this would happen. After considerable thought he decided that the thing to do was to build bunkhouses in each of the block-and-tackles. These were as large as the foc's'le on the old *Silver Maid*. In the end, a small bunkhouse was tucked into the blocks at the end of each yardarm, and the men were able to reach their posts promptly at every sudden squall.

Another difficulty which the *Tuscarora* encountered on her first voyage was that of getting stuck in the clouds. On one occasion, as a matter of fact, her upper topgallants caught in the sickle of a low-hanging new moon. For a moment it was touch-and-go whether the *Tuscarora* would pull the moon out of the sky, or the moon slice through the *Tuscarora's* rigging. But Stormalong skillfully maneuvered the ship to slip out of the tangle. This, of course, could have been dangerous in a brisk wind. Stormy suggested, consequently, that the masts be hinged, so that they could be folded down under the constellations of stars and heavenly bodies, like the funnels of a tug under a low bridge.

These were the only structural changes he recommended. His other suggestions had to do chiefly with the comfort of his men.

It was almost impossible for the young officers to reach their stations during their watches, the distances were so great. As much as he hated to do it, Stormalong decided to keep a stable of Arab ponies on deck. Many old-time sailors still clung to the superstition that horses on a ship bring bad luck, but the *Tuscarora* was no place for old-fashioned superstitions.

It was obvious to Captain Stormalong that an ordinary crew would not be able to handle the ship in a rough sea. At least a thousand hands were required, eight hundred able-bodied seamen, twenty mates, including four first mates,

and Heaven knew how many other officers, cabin boys, galley hands, carpenters, sailmakers, and so on. Feeding this crew was more than had ever been attempted in the merchant marine. Porky knew he could handle the cooking, but he would need the proper equipment. They spent many hours trying to work out this problem.

One evening, as Stormy sat in the galley finishing off a section of Barnacle Pie, his eye was caught by a group of galley boys. They were having their troubles tossing peeled onions over their heads into the soup kettle on top of the stove. The smaller ones were barely able to heave the smelly vegetables over the rim of the high pot.

"Cook!" the Captain bellowed. "Come here!"

Adolphus Don Sebastian Whittier Green, otherwise known as Porky, shivered in his boots. For all he knew, the Old Man had broken a tooth on the contents of his pie.

"Come here, Cookie!" Stormy shouted again. "I've got it! I know what's wrong with this galley!" Without thinking, he slapped Porky on the back with a blow that sent the latter crashing into the china cupboard.

When Porky had been dusted off and comforted, the two of them sat down at the long mess table, while Stormalong sketched his ideas on the cloth. "Here . . . here . . . here . . . !" he murmured, chiefly to himself, as his pencil dug into the clean linen.

"Yes, but . . . here . . . !" Porky interjected once or twice, in full agreement with his captain's notions, but with a more intimate knowledge of cooking.

The galley was finally built amidships, with hatches in the roof. Beneath these hatches were ten huge kettles for cooking stews and chowders. The vegetables were peeled and the fish were cleaned on deck and dropped into the boiling water below. Ten tremendous cookstoves, joined into one, were constructed on a downhill slope. At the upper end, the oven door opened to receive the huge pans of Barnacle Pie which Porky and his twenty assistants placed inside. By the time these reached the lower oven door, the pies were baked brown. In the same way, skillets of frying fish and flapjacks were placed on top of the stove at the upper end. The slope was so gentle that the food was crisp and golden by the time the skillets had slid to the bottom. A permanent coffee kettle the size of a small furnace was installed, with pipes leading out to all parts of the ship. In this way, it was possible for the officers and the men to have hot coffee whenever they wished it, without exhausting a relay of galley boys.

These modern improvements in the galley left no room for the men to sit down to their meals. At first, Stormalong decided to have them eat in shifts. He tried this out on the test voyage. It worked after a fashion, but the second shift had to wait until lunchtime while the galley boys washed the breakfast dishes of the first shift.

The solution proved to be simple enough. Stormy gave each member of the crew a tin plate, a cup, and the necessary cutlery. They could fill their plates as they passed the windows of the galley near the lower end of the stove. By the time the last sailor had had breakfast, the first was ready for lunch, and so on. Someone was always being fed. No one, therefore, would go hungry. This proved to be an excellent idea. After several years of its success on the

Tuscarora, the idea was copied by a landlubber. He claimed the credit for inventing the cafeteria.

At long last, the ship was properly fitted out. Each of Stormalong's recommendations were acted upon.

Just before the *Tuscarora* sailed on her maiden voyage, Toby added the finishing touch. He suggested that the Statue of Liberty be taken down from New York Harbor and used as a figurehead for the ship. Stormalong was too modest and patriotic to permit such a thing. Besides, the Statue was too heavy for the delicate balance of the craft. Toby contented himself with having a life-size copy carved out of balsam wood, so that all the harbors of the world might see Miss Liberty at the prow of the greatest Yankee vessel of them all.

CHAPTER SEVEN

The White Cliffs
of Dover

*I*F A SHIP CAN BE SAID TO
have feelings, the *Tuscarora* had them. She sensed Stormalong's every whim before he could put it into a thought.
She responded to his moods as a favorite mare responds to
a hunter's nudges.

With Stormy at the wheel, the *Tuscarora* was the swiftest,
the steadiest ship on the seas. She could perform in any
kind of weather so smoothly that no one, not even the
greenest cabin boy, was ever known to be seasick. One
evening, for instance, Porky came up on deck from his galley
to find out when they were scheduled to sail. To his surprise, he learned that they had left Boston four days before
and were riding out a wild North Atlantic gale off the coast
of Iceland. Mountainous black waves were gently caressing
the *Tuscarora's* hull. She was not even shipping water. As a
matter of fact, several of the crew were having an off-duty
game of shuffleboard on the forward deck.

It would not be correct to give the impression that the
Tuscarora had a completely uneventful history. Her great

size created many unusual situations. There were few harbors which could accomodate her. She was frequently forced to anchor in deep water miles off the coast. Small fleets of clipper ships were engaged as tenders, to load and unload her cargo. At first, this seemed to be a disadvantage. Toby pointed out to Stormy, however, that the circumstance could be turned to good account. If the ship were anchored in the Gulf of Mexico, for instance, she could take on and discharge cargo for several ports at once. Her tenders could work back and forth from New Orleans, Galveston, Mobile, and other smaller cities at the same time. This would cut out the need for many coastwise trips.

The *Tuscarora* was subject to the accidents that happen to any vessel. She had once taken on a load of elephants from the Belgian Congo for Barnum and Bailey's circus. The Second First Mate, then at the wheel, failed to allow enough room for the ship to turn around as she headed out of the Gulf of Guinea. He held his course too close to shore off the Dark Continent, which was difficult to distinguish in the black tropical night. The ship scraped bottom on the rocks off the Gold Coast. A large hole was torn in her hull on the starboard side. Water gushed into the hold where the elephants were housed.

There was little danger that the *Tuscarora* would sink. Her holds had been designed for just such accidents, each a watertight compartment in itself. The only real danger was that the cargo in the damaged compartment might be ruined.

Live elephants are a precious cargo. They are, furthermore, excitable creatures, likely to stampede at the slightest change in their routine. As the water swirled about their chained feet, the great beasts lost their heads. They set up a trumpeting and a screaming that threatened to shake the *Tuscarora* to bits. Captain Stormalong rushed to survey the situation and ordered a hundred men to man the pumps. Work as they might, they could not stop the water, which now was gushing in with force.

The hullabaloo was at its peak when Stormy caught the eye of Old Tusco, the King of the Elephants. Tusco had ruled the herd in the Upper Congo Valley for many years. He was widely known for his sensible approach to critical situations. He beckoned to Stormalong, whom he recognized as a fellow leader. The two leaders conferred briefly.

JOSHUA TOLFORD

Then Stormy gave the order, "Remove the chains from these elephants!"

Quietly, without any sign of panic, old Tusco moved to the breach in the wall, sucked up a trunkful of water, and squirted it out into the night. The other elephants paused in their confused bellowing and stomping. They had faith in Tusco and were struck by his calm manner. As soon as they recognized what he was doing, their panic disappeared.

One by one they began to imitate him. In no time at all, the pumping crews, assisted by two hundred and fifty elephants, cleared the flooded hold. A patch was made in the ship's side. She sped across the Atlantic without further accident. For the remainder of the voyage, old Tusco took his meals as Stormalong's guest in the Captain's cabin. The two became firm friends.

Some of the *Tuscarora's* adventures were less happy than the episode of the elephants. On one of her voyages she was threatened with destruction three times within a matter of days. Returning from a routine run to Capetown, she was ordered to stop at Stockholm in the Baltic Sea for a cargo of pickled herring.

Stormalong examined his charts carefully. He realized that the run might involve a tight squeeze in the Kattegat, that narrow strait of water between Denmark and Sweden. Some of his officers, moreover, were alarmed by the reports of the giant kraken, a mysterious under-water beast which was said to live in the waters off the coast of Norway.

The giant kraken is related to the octopus. He is, in fact, one of the few remaining examples of a pre-historic branch of the family. In shape he vaguely resembles a crab, with

a hard, armored shell a mile and a half in circumference over the mass of his body. This shell is of a mottled dark green which blends with the dark green of deep sea water. He is practically invisible, even to the trained eyes of Scandinavian sailors. His great tentacles, like giant lobster claws, extend from the sides of the shell. He is not a pretty beast.

His habits are even less attractive than his appearance. Although he lives at the bottom of the sea, eighty to one hundred fathoms below the surface, he likes to vary his diet with such delicacies as flocks of sea-gulls and fishing dories with their crews. At unpredictable intervals he rises to the surface to indulge himself in these dainties. Whenever he rises, the water swirls and eddies for miles around, like shoal water. When he submerges, the suction creates a tremendous whirlpool that can pull large ships down into seething destruction.

Out in the open waters of the North Sea, where uncharted shoals give warning that the kraken is active, there is not

JOSHUA TOLFORD

too much danger. A fast ship can change course in time to sail around the critical area. In a narrow body of water like the Kattegat, however, the kraken can be difficult indeed.

Stormalong listened to the tales his officers had to tell and thought about the matter. He himself had often heard tales of its existence. He recalled other terrors of the sea, however, which he had overcome. Among them he recalled his fight with the octopus in the West Indies. He had been hardly more than a boy when that took place! He thought, too, about his wild ride across the Pacific on the back of a great white whale. No serious damage had come of that!

On the basis of these recollections and with the knowledge that the *Tuscarora* was the most manageable ship afloat, he decided not to worry about the kraken. He had, furthermore, set his heart on a good breakfast of pickled herring! He ordered the course set for Stockholm!

The *Tuscarora* had just passed the great beacon of the Naze when queer things began to happen. Whirlpools and eddies appeared for no good reason in the deepest water of the channel. A rip tide caught the ship and almost whirled her around, while a gust of wind threatened to drive her on the rocks of the Norwegian coast. Stormalong kept the wheel firmly in hand. The *Tuscarora* stubbornly held to her course. The Bosun was frightened as he took his soundings. He was well acquainted with these waters, and knew that the channel should be fifty fathoms deep. Each time a whirlpool appeared, however, the water grew more shallow.

"Twenty fathoms," he sang out, "eighteen fathoms . . . fifteen fathoms . . . twelve fathoms . . .!" The pitch of his voice grew higher with each announcement. Stormalong chuckled to himself. He knew that he had met the kraken and that the *Tuscarora* was equal to the situation.

"All hands on deck!" he shouted. "Get up the topmast stuns'ls! Crowd the canvas on her! What she can't carry, she'll have to drag!"

The crew sprang to the rigging. The *Tuscarora* leaped through the water, her slim bow slipping through the choppy sea like a snake through a stand of grasses. Then, as a well-trained hunter jumps over a wall, the *Tuscarora* cleared the back of the kraken and settled herself in the calm water of the channel.

She made a ninety-degree turn as Stormalong quickly flipped the wheel and headed her around the Skaw, the pointed tip of Denmark which separates the Skagerrak from the Kattegat. The impetus of the dash over the kraken's back carried the ship through the straits of Elsinore. She was safely at anchor off Stockholm by the next morning.

Stormalong spent a pleasant evening in Stockholm recounting his adventures to a pair of Swedish captains whom he had met on visits to the Chinese ports. These men were much interested in the story. They assured Stormalong that few ships had been as lucky as the *Tuscarora*.

In addition to the twenty thousand barrels of pickled herring, Stormy took on a load of Swedish steel, which he happened to pick up at a bargain. The *Tuscarora* rode low in the water under the weight of her cargo as she set out on her return from Stockholm. The Captain himself kept the wheel to carry her past the narrow waters of the Kattegat and out into the feeding grounds of the kraken. They had just cleared the Skagerrak when the first evidence of the lurking beast appeared. The ground swell broke into white-caps, the waters swirled with an ominous rhythm, and the Bosun's soundings showed shoal water where no shoals were charted. The Captain prepared to use the same tactics he had used successfully once before. He was about to order all hands aloft when the wind died.

Stormalong had not counted upon this. The swirling of the waters slowed to a lazy pace. This was proof that the kraken was aware of the dying of the wind. The *Tuscarora* was becalmed directly above the back of the monster and completely at its mercy!

The Bosun shrieked his soundings frantically. "Ten fathoms! . . . Lord have mercy! . . . Eight fathoms! . . . Seven fathoms! . . . Six fathoms! . . . Save us!" He begged the Captain to throw the steel overboard in the hopes that the ship would ride more lightly and be able to get away.

Stormalong was well aware of the dangers immediately ahead. He blamed himself for being overconfident. He should have listened more carefully to his friends the Swedish captains. Better still, he should not have attempted the trip in the first place. The *Tuscarora* was a ship for the open ocean. Penned up in a little sea, she could not maneuver freely. His thoughtless pride had placed her and all her loyal crew in jeopardy. It was up to him to get her out of the difficulty.

Stormy carefully checked the distances between the whirlpools on the surface of the water. He checked the Bosun's soundings and the color of the sea. He figured that the neck of the kraken lay half a mile ahead and would soon emerge.

There was only one chance to take, and he was the only one who could take it.

He stripped off his coat and his cap and leaped to the foc's'le. "Open the gear locker!" he shouted to the Mate. "Break out the biggest harpoon we carry!"

The heavy iron was dragged forward and Stormy coiled the line at his feet. He braced himself and kept his eyes on the horizon. Just as he had guessed, an ugly snout broke through the water half a mile in front of the ship's bow, spouting contemptuously into the air. Stormy's eyes narrowed with anger when the monster challenged him to the duel. His huge right arm swung back in a great arc, then forward. The harpoon whistled through the air and buried itself in the kraken's neck.

"All hands aloft! Prepare to crowd on sail!" roared Stormalong, as the kraken recovered from the shock. The monster writhed and wriggled, lashed his tentacles. He tried to shake off the harpoon and fling the ship against the cliffs of Stavanger. But Stormalong held on. In a last desperate effort, the kraken dove into the depths.

Stormy had been waiting for this. The watery walls of the great funnel which opened behind the kraken whirled at a tremendous speed. The *Tuscarora* raced around the edge of the crater, barely keeping its balance. Slowly and carefully, Stormy played out the line of the harpoon until at last he let it go entirely. The ship shot off the crater from the centrifugal force of its whirling and cleared the treacherous area of the whirlpool. The sailors quickly unfurled the canvas, just in time to catch a fresh breeze, and the *Tuscarora*, safe again, settled in the bosom of the North Sea.

It had been a close call, but Stormalong had saved the day!

The crew felt that there had been enough excitement for one voyage. But the *Tuscarora's* troubles were not over. The fresh breeze died suddenly. A fog blanketed the ocean. Usually a fog at sea is accompanied by calm water, but not this one. The North Sea heaved and tossed alarmingly as the death throes of the kraken made themselves felt.

Meanwhile the fog grew worse and worse. It was so thick the men had to cut paths with axes in order to reach their stations. It was impossible to tell where the fog ended and the sea began. Even the fish were confused. One of the junior officers ran headlong into a school of deep-sea bass, who had lost their way and were swimming blindly on the afterdeck. When Hammerhead went below after his watch, he found a family of mackerel snuggled comfortably in his bunk.

At last the fog cleared. The *Tuscarora* had indeed worked herself into a tight spot. She had been swept into the narrow end of the North Sea, between England and Holland. As luck would have it, she was heading southwest by west. Directly ahead of her loomed the Straits of Dover.

At their narrowest, between Folkestone and Calais, the Straits measure about twenty miles wide. This was roughly the width of the *Tuscarora* amidships. There was obviously no room in which the ship could be turned around in order to leave the North Sea through the open waters north of Scotland. The prevailing wind was north-northeast. Any effort to back the ship into a wider channel would be unsuccessful. Stormalong called a conference of all his officers.

The meeting in the Captain's cabin was short. When the men emerged, Stormy gave an order to drop anchor and put the lifeboats over the port side. The officers retired to their cabins, and quickly returned to the deck in their best dress uniforms. Five thousand barrels of pickled herrings were lowered into the lifeboats along with the officers. The little fleet headed for the Hague on the Dutch shore.

As everyone knows, the Dutch are among the cleanest and tidiest people on earth. In order to keep their houses shining and their faces glistening, they need soap — and plenty of it! They are also very fond of pickled herring.

Stormalong's officers went straight to the town hall and explained their predicament to the city fathers. The good Dutch burghers listened sympathetically. They were, for the most part, merchants and seafaring men themselves.

They had long known and admired the reputation of Captain Stormalong and were happy to help him in his hour of need. At first they refused the gift of pickled herring. But they were finally persuaded to accept it.

Couriers were sent to every nook and corner of Holland, and to a few selected border towns in Belgium. Everywhere housewives opened their cupboards and gave up their stores of soap. Delicately perfumed face soap, harsh scrubbing soap, laundry soap, shaving soap, and even scouring powder, were loaded into dogcarts and trundled to the boats waiting in the harbor of The Hague. The coast of Holland was jammed with sightseers, who came with their families and picnic baskets to watch the operation.

Once the soap had been taken aboard the *Tuscarora*, Stormy put the men to work. The crew were let down over

the sides in bosun's chairs, each man with a brush and a bucket of soap jelly. They spread the soap as thick as they could over the hull. At the end of a long day's work, the *Tuscarora* was smeared from stem to stern with a slippery coating. Little froths of suds, like a lace edging, encircled her water-line.

When the work was completed, Stormalong ordered the anchor hauled up, the canvas unfurled. Taking advantage of a brisk wind, he urged the ship forward into the narrow straits. It was a tight squeeze! The picnicking Dutchmen on the shore joined the crew in a loud cheer as the *Tuscarora* slipped through the narrow bottle-neck and cleared her way into the English Channel out onto the broad Atlantic.

Phew! said Stormy to himself, as he realized he was at last headed home after an eventful voyage.

JOSHUA TOLFORD

The choppy waters of the Channel washed a good bit of the soap off the ship's sides. For weeks thereafter clouds of iridescent soap bubbles rose into the sky like round rainbows whenever the wind freshened. Bubbles are temporary things at best, however, and in time these were forgotten.

One permanent souvenir of the incident remained. As the *Tuscarora* squeezed through the narrowest channel, her starboard rail brushed against the cliffs on the British coast. The soap on that side was scraped off by the jutting rocks. To this day it remains there. It stands out white and clear, and has become a famous landmark for tourists. The headlands, which had before been a sandy red, were now the color of chalk. They have been known ever since as the White Cliffs of Dover.

CHAPTER EIGHT

Inventions

and Discoveries

*B*Y *SOLVING THE PROBLEMS*
which confronted the *Tuscarora*, Stormalong and Toby were
responsible for many inventions and discoveries for which
neither has ever received proper credit.

One problem of primary importance was that of pro-
viding fresh drinking water for the crew of the ship. She was
so large, and her crew so numerous, that she needed as much
water as the city of Boston itself. It took a whole pond to
fill her tanks. On her first trip, Fresh Pond in Cambridge
had been drained. Even so, she had to stop off the coast of
Iceland to replenish her drinking-water from a glacial river.

At last Stormalong thought of a way to keep the *Tuscarora*
supplied without interrupting her voyages. He added an
extra topmast above the skysail and had it sharpened to a
needle-point. Whenever his water supply showed signs of
drying up, he maneuvered the ship under the nearest thundercloud. The fine tip of the topmast pierced the cloud and
caused a shower of rain which filled the open tanks on the
deck. The technique has since been applied with some suc-

cess by scientists trying to make rain. Instead of sailing under a cloud with a sharpened topmast, however, they sail over it in a plane and pierce it from above with little pellets of dry ice. The effect is much the same.

One spring day the *Tuscarora* sailed directly into the path of a typhoon in the Indian Ocean. For four long nights and days the battle raged. The ship kept doggedly on her course in spite of high seas and treacherous winds. The typhoon tried all its most murderous tricks. Stormalong held the wheel firmly, and by sunset of the fourth day the typhoon admitted defeat. It was exhausted.

In itself, the battle was not important. The *Tuscarora* and her doughty skipper had been through worse storms. A great idea entered Stormalong's mind, nevertheless, when he saw the typhoon in its worn-out condition. It had been reduced to nothing more than a gentle, passive, whimpering breeze.

Stormy had for months been concerned about the lack of fresh air below decks. If only he could induce some tired gale to blow gently through the holds, his crew would be much more comfortable. This seemed to be his chance.

He called Olaf the Big Norwegian, who was now chief ship's carpenter and naval architect, into his cabin. Together they unrolled the blueprints of the *Tuscarora* and Stormy spread them on the chart table. He inked in a general outline for a system of ducts and shafts to run the length and breadth of the ship. It was all Olaf could do to follow on his hands and knees the swift, sure dashes of Stormalong's quill pen. At last the specifications were worked out.

Olaf called his men together and set about the work itself.

The clanging of saws and hammers made a noisy racket. Stormalong was so absorbed in the project that he failed to notice what was happening off the afterdeck.

The typhoon, which had followed the ship listlessly, like a captive in chains, had become ill. The noise of the building going on aboard the *Tuscarora* added to its misery. Pale, feeble, frightened, it breathed its last, without even disturbing the ship's wake. When Olaf had finished his work and the time had come to put the Captain's scheme into action, there was not so much as the ghost of a zephyr left to wander through the new ventilating system.

At first Stormy was angry that the typhoon had cheated him of his success. His anger, however, soon gave way to pity, and this, in turn, was replaced with pleasure when he realized that fresh air was indeed blowing through the new ducts. The forward speed of the *Tuscarora* forced a steady breeze into the intake in the prow. The suction created by her passing pulled it out again through the outlet in the stern.

One of Stormalong's more resourceful actions had consequences which could not possibly have been foreseen by anyone, least of all by Stormy. He and the *Tuscarora* had been dispatched to the West Coast for a cargo of smoked salmon. A year before, a merchantman, carrying prospectors to the California Gold Rush, had brought back to Boston a keg of smoked salmon. The pretty pink color of the flesh and the delightful new flavor caught the fancy of the lucky few who sampled it. It was much tastier than dried cod, of which New Englnaders were growing very tired. Immediately there was a great demand for the Pacific fish.

When the *Tuscarora* anchored off the mouth of the Columbia River, Stormy sent his messengers to Astoria to bid for the salmon catch of the area. To his dismay, the men returned with sad news. Drying and smoking salmon is a slow business. To complete the order, the native Indians needed four years and seven months and fifteen days, according to the shortest estimate. This would tie up the big ship for a long, unprofitable waste of time.

Stormalong was tempted to return to Boston empty-handed and to explain that the commission had not been practicable. Before he gave in to this temptation, however, he was invited to dinner by the Mayor of Astoria. The main course of the meal comprised fresh salmon steak, a delicacy which Stormy had never before tasted. He knew this would go like hot cakes in the East. How to transport fresh salmon — this became his problem!

He spent a week ashore, studying the methods of the salmon fishermen and the habits of the fish themselves. He watched the shiny silvery bodies flash up over the rapids as they made their way upstream from the ocean to the spawning grounds in the upper Columbia River. An idea began to take form in his mind. After a brief consultation with the mayor, Stormalong ordered all the fishing nets in the area lashed together to form a giant weir. This stretched between Cape Disappointment on the northern tip of Columbia River Bay to Point Adams on the southern limit.

In no time at all the river as far as Astoria was filled with sleek, silvery, shining bodies. Stormy's men could walk from one side of the river mouth to the other without getting their feet wet.

Captain Stormalong ordered the *Tuscarora's* hatches opened. With great shovels the men scooped the squirming cargo aboard until the holds were two-thirds filled.

"Stop!" Stormy roared suddenly through his megaphone. "Close the hatches! Prepare to embark!"

The junior officers looked at each other in dismay. They could think only of the long voyage ahead through hot Equatorial waters. They shuddered to think of the results of one day in the Torrid Zone with the holds full of fresh fish. An impertinent midshipman clutched his nose between his thumb and forefinger. Several of his companions followed suit.

"*Mis*ter Jones! *Mis*ter Brown! *Mis*ter Peabody!" The Captain's roar echoed and re-echoed against the galley wall where the lads were standing. "*This* will be enough of your mutinous nonsense! To your quarters, gentlemen!"

The midshipmen obeyed Stormalong's order meekly. They whispered among themselves that the Old Man had gone mad, completely mad. As the last of them reached the companionway to the lower deck, he heard Stormy sing out the order,

"Hoist the anchor! Helmsman, set the course north by northwest!"

Then indeed the midshipmen knew the Old Man had lost his mind. He apparently intended to go home by way of the Arctic Sea. No one had ever found a way from the West to the East across the northern limits of the American continent. The junior officers had begun to consider a proper mutiny, when a field of icebergs was sighted off the entrance to the Bering Strait.

Stormalong now took the most amazing course of his career. A reasonable ship's captain would avoid an iceberg field like the plague. But not Captain A. B. Stormalong! A giant berg loomed immediately forward off the port bow. Instead of veering to starboard, Stormy turned the wheel to port directly into the mass of shimmering ice. Officers, midshipmen and sailors were paralyzed! Certain destruction was all they could foresee.

"Heave to!" barked the Captain's order.

No one dared to move.

"Don't stand there like idiots!" Stormy snapped. "Heave to! Throw out the grapples!"

This time the men obeyed his order. The ship came to rest in a hollow in the ice.

"Now break out the picks and axes! Open the hatches!" Stormy's command rang out.

The reasoning behind the Old Man's strange behavior became clear when the carpenters and sailmakers were ordered over the side to chip out blocks of ice. The remainder of the crew formed a bucket brigade which passed the ice into the open hatches. Before sundown the iceberg had been broken into chunks and stowed below the *Tuscarora's* decks to keep the salmon fresh on her long voyage home.

The crew, greatly relieved, cheered as the helmsman turned the big ship around in the Aleutian Archipelago and headed for Boston.

This method of preserving a perishable cargo had never been tried before. Stormy's resourcefulness was in fact the first application of refrigeration to merchant shipping. The *Tuscarora* had, among her other claims to fame, the distinc-

tion of being the first refrigerator ship, or "reefer," as the
class is known in shipping circles.

Back in New England, Stormalong and Toby had no
trouble selling the fabulous cargo of the *Tuscarora*, but
when it came to disposing of the ice, that was a different
matter! There was obviously no market for ice in New England. Every little township had its pond and ice-house. The
large chunks left in the ship's hold, furthermore, could not
be dumped into Massachusetts Bay for fear of endangering
the small craft of the fishing fleet.

Toby suggested that the *Tuscarora* dump her cargo in the
icefields off Greenland. This did not appeal to Stormalong
who disliked to make an essentially unprofitable voyage if
he could help it. Toby made other suggestions, but Storm

106

found fault with each of them. At last, with some impatience, Toby reminded Stormy that it was *his* doing which had saddled them with the problem. Perhaps *he* could think of a satisfactory way out. The friendship of the two men was in danger of being strained, when the same idea struck them both at once.

Of course! Why hadn't they thought of it before! The Tropics had no ice! Even a small chunk would bring a large price from the perspiring inhabitants of the Caribbean countries. They clapped each other on the shoulders. The even tenor of their friendship was restored!

It was June when Stormy started South with his chilly cargo. Off Cape Hatteras he ran into a warm breeze and the ice began to melt. In order to gain time, he ordered the crew to crowd on the canvas. Every inch of yardarm was decked with sail when the *Tuscarora* turned into the Caribbean Sea.

Unfortunately, a sullen little hurricane was lurking there. The ship had no sooner cleared the Florida Keys when the storm pounced without warning before the sails could be furled. Decked out as she was, the *Tuscarora* was caught up in the winds and fell to their mercy. All Stormalong could do was to hold the wheel and try to direct her passage. It was impossible to stop her headlong dash against the coast of the Americas.

With great presence of mind, Stormy recalled a narrow stretch of land between North and South America. This was Panama. The Isthmus was so narrow and the speed of the ship so great, Stormy thought perhaps her momentum would carry her over the land into the Pacific. At least, this was his only hope. He turned the *Tuscarora's* prow toward the Panama shore.

As he expected, the hurricane lifted the ship out of the water and carried her over the narrow neck of land. He missed his goal, however. The force was not great enough to carry the heavy *Tuscarora* all the way to the Pacific Ocean. Instead, she settled in the waters of a large swamp, known as Miraflores Lake. In her flight her keel had cut a deep gash across the Isthmus, but the ship itself was not injured. She was, however, grounded in the heart of the jungle.

Stormalong surveyed the situation. Miraflores Lake is on the Pacific side of the Continental Divide. To return to the Atlantic Ocean, even if the gash cut by the ship's keel could be deepened, would be a heartbreaking chore. Between Miraflores Lake and the Pacific Ocean, however, the land ran down hill. The distance was not far. If he could dig a ditch to the Pacific, he might be able to float the *Tuscarora* out. He then began to figure on the back of an old envelope. His whole crew, digging at top speed, would need almost a year to complete a satisfactory channel. This was too long. He needed outside help.

As he stood looking at the Western Sea, thinking, a strange phenomenon occurred in the forests around the edge of the lake in which the ship rested. Brilliant patches of color twinkled and flashed behind the trees of the jungle. Stormalong became aware that he was being watched. And yet all was silent. Not a twig crackled. It was an eerie situation, as though the jungle were bewitched.

Stormy was never one to put up with an unknown quantity. He preferred to find out what was going on. He climbed

down the *Tuscarora's* ladder, strode to the edge of the for.
est, and there saw scores of backs, covered in beautifully
feathered capes, disappearing into the wilderness.

Panamanian Indians! he laughed to himself.

These shy creatures had crept to the edge of the jungle to
peer at the huge white eagle that had settled on their lake
At Stormy's approach they were frightened away. His problem was solved, however. Here was the help he needed.

Stormy hurried back to the *Tuscarora* and called together
his most versatile officers. He then despatched them to seek
out the chief of the Indians. In a litter borne by four men
they carried with them Stormalong's silver shaving mug, as
a present for the Indian chieftain. Better still, they also carried ice in buckets slung from poles over their shoulders.

Their mission was successful. The high chieftain was flat-
tered and delighted at the present of the shaving mug. He
placed it in the center of his village as a fountain, in imita-
tion of the Spanish cities of Mexico and Peru. He was even
more pleased with the ice. He thought it was magic. Never
before had he seen or touched anything so wonderfully cold
in all his years in the tropical jungle. He offered all his wives
to help dig the ditch.

When he understood that more help still was needed, he
sent for his wives' brothers and fathers. Captain Stormalong
saw that each of the Indians was paid for his labors in ice.
This was such a rare treat that word spread quickly throughout Central America and the Caribbean countries. Indians
from Colombia, Costa Rica, Nicaragua, El Salvador, Hon-
duras, and from as far north as Guatamala and the jungles
of Yucatan, flocked to the scene to take part in the digging

and to taste the ice. Within two months the ditch was completed. The waters of Lake Miraflores rushed into it. The *Tuscarora* floated majestically out into the Pacific Ocean. As a token of gratitude, Stormalong ordered whatever ice remained in the ship's hull poured out into the bed of the lake for the use of his friends the Indians.

The story has been told that a party of Army engineers happened to be in the neighborhood when the *Tuscarora* made her mad dash across the Panama Isthmus. They are said to have followed the cut it made through the jungle hills and to have watched from hiding the digging of the ditch to the Pacific. The tale goes on that they hurried back to Washington and claimed that they had built the Panama Canal.

This is not true at all! Stormalong had long since been gathered to the bosom of the sea when the Army began to look for a suitable place to build a canal across the Continent. When the surveyors reached Panama, they found the old cut and the ditch, grown over with moss and jungle foliage. They recognized, however, that a beginning had been made, which would simplify the work enormously. Therefore they recommended that Stormalong's old track be cleaned up, deepened, and widened. *This* is the proper version of the story of the origin of the Panama Canal.

CHAPTER NINE

Tempests and Teakettles

*N*O MATTER WHAT CAPTAIN
A. B. Stormalong achieved, he was never satisfied with things
as they were. He believed, above all, in progress. The only
limit to his imagination was that progress had to be *natural*
progress. He was forever seeking ways of taming the forces
of Nature to work for him.

His experience in Panama convinced him that something
had to be done about the weather. As he reviewed his career, he realized that all his mishaps, which had fortunately
never been serious, arose from the fact that he could not
foretell the time or the place at which a storm would strike.
When he returned to Boston he discussed the problem with
Toby.

As one of the *Tuscarora's* owners, Toby had a personal
interest in seeing that voyages went smoothly. He sent his
secretary, a young intelligent boy just out of Harvard, to the
Boston Athenaeum to see what could be learned about fore-
casting storms. The secretary returned after a week of poking about in the library. He carried with him two volumes

—— one, an account of Aristotle's efforts to forecast weather in the fourth century, B.C., and the other, a copy of the *Old Farmer's Almanack*. Neither of these was of any assistance. For a time it looked as though the problem could not be solved.

On his next voyage, Stormalong spent long hours thinking. He watched the sea and its creatures. There are many signs given to an observant mariner by Nature. A hazy circle around the moon foretells rain to come. A sun-dog, a great misty circle around the sun, foretells a hurricane. Whenever a storm is brewing, the cockles and other shellfish fill their shells with sand for ballast. Dolphins and porpoises, too, can be used as indications. They come from the direction of the wind and their behavior gives a clue to future weather. If they jump and frisk about in the water, a gale is on its way. On the other hand, if they swim forward in a dignified procession, there is calm weather ahead.

All these signs helped, of course, but they were limited. Stormalong still could not tell when a gale would strike, at least in time to prepare the *Tuscarora* to ride it out without discomfort.

At last his genius asserted itself. Among the creatures on whom he relied for storm warnings was a bird, the stormy petrel. Sailors sometimes call these friendly birds "Mother Carey's chickens." They are also called tempest birds, because their presence in great numbers around a ship is thought to mean storms to come. They often follow a craft for hundreds of miles at sea, picking up the crumbs which are thrown overboard from the galleys.

Stormalong had never paid much attention to them until

he noticed a flock of *pintadoes,* or Cape Pigeons. This is a variety of petrel found in the region of the Cape of Good Hope. He was struck by their resemblance to the pigeons he himself had fed in Boston Common. He recalled, too, an article in the *Atlantic Monthly* concerning the use of homing pigeons to carry messages. Toby had called his attention to it. Why not train petrels to carry reports about the weather?

Stormalong worked patiently for many months developing his idea. He had messes of fish thrown over the afterdeck rail morning and night to the flocks. As they squabbled over the dainty morsels, he picked out the strongest and most intelligent of the birds. These he coaxed aboard with specially tempting tidbits. At last he made friends with the leaders. With their assistance, he started a training program.

Within a year he had two thousand well-educated petrels in cages on the afterdeck of the *Tuscarora.* Groups of these were sent out each morning, each bird with a specially colored band on his leg and headed toward a particular point of the compass. If a bird returned with his feathers ruffled, Stormy knew the petrel had hit rough weather. From the color of the leg band, he could tell the storm's direction. By timing the bird's absence from the ship, he could tell the storm's exact distance.

Other petrels were trained to fly to the home port of Boston from all corners of the earth. One of these was dispatched to Toby's office every morning and one every evening, with a complete weather report banded to his leg.

This service was of great value to the owners, who were

thus enabled to warn the other ships of their line about storms and hurricanes. They patriotically shared their information with the United States Government, for the use of the Coast Guard and the Navy. The Government was delighted, and set up a special office to develop Stormalong's idea even further. This has since become known as the United States Weather Bureau.

Stormalong's own achievements did not blind him to the success of other men. He was generous with his praise of others who, like himself, used and developed natural forces.

Among these was Donald McKay, the architect of the Yankee clipper ships.

The clippers were beautiful ships, trim and swift. They were developed to the point where they could outrun any craft on the high seas, with the obvious exception of the *Tuscarora*. Their competition did not worry Stormy. He knew McKay had borrowed some of his own ideas in designing the sleek new greyhounds of the ocean. He had given full permission. His only regret was that he himself was too large to handle one of them. He used to stand on the wharf at McKay's shipyard to watch the little beauties slipping about the harbor.

When the *Flying Cloud,* the finest clipper of them all, broke the record for the run between New York and San Francisco with a voyage of eighty-nine days and twenty-one minutes, Stormalong took her challenge indulgently as a friendly one. He set out to prove to his own satisfaction that the *Tuscarora* could cut the time in half. He redesigned her rigging to allow more canvas. He added an extra skysail and a moonraker on each of her mainmasts. He trimmed her lines by dropping her lifeboats and stabling the officer's Arab ponies below the deck.

It was a bitter winter day when the *Tuscarora* chose to sail out of New York to beat the *Flying Cloud's* record. The rigging was encased in ice. The temperature was five below zero. A fierce wintry blast filled the ship's sails. The men of the crew stood by their posts until Sandy Hook had been cleared and the course set for the south. Several then went below to fetch extra woolen mufflers to wrap around their faces. To their surprise, when they returned to the deck, they realized that the *Tuscarora* was off the Bahamas. A hot tropical sun blazed directly overhead, blistering the paint on her decks. The *Flying Cloud* had needed twenty-one days to reach the Equator. There was no doubt that the *Tuscarora* would win the race with ease.

When the big ship reached San Francisco, Stormalong allowed her to pause only momentarily. He took time enough to write down on a small slip of paper the exact time of his arrival. This was notarized by the Governor of California. Stormy bound the slip to the leg of his swiftest homing petrel and released the bird to fly East across the continent to tell Toby of the ship's achievement. He then turned the ship around and started home.

The petrel unfortunately ran into difficulty over the Rocky Mountains. A headwind slowed its flight. For a time it lost its bearings and followed the Colorado River, in the mistaken notion that it was following the Missouri River eastward. As soon as it reached the Grand Canyon, it realized its mistake and changed course. Even so, it was too late. The *Tuscarora* reached New York before the petrel.

Thanks to this accident, certain sceptical New Yorkers refused to believe Stormy's claim of beating the *Flying Cloud's* record. They insisted that he had simply taken the *Tuscarora* down to Barnegat Bay and back, and that someone else had released the petrel. How did they know the Governor of California's signature when they saw it? It might have been written by the Mayor of Philadelphia. They refused to make an official record in the Shipping News column of the *Times,* and the event was thereby lost to history. Stormalong, however, did not mind. He had no wish for personal glory. It was enough for him to know certainly that the *Tuscarora* was still the fastest ship on the high seas.

For some time he was content. Not for long, however! More and more when he settled with his friends for an evening's conversation, the subject of steam shipping cropped up. Steam shipping indeed!

This was the kind of progress for which Stormalong had no use. Wind and canvas, the strength of men's arms and the skill in their heads — these were the only basic elements needed to speed a ship through ocean water. He had no patience with "lazy good-for-nothings" who wanted to make the boiling water in their grandmothers' teakettles run a ship. The idea was *unnatural!* Besides, it wouldn't work!

Stormalong pointed to the experiment made by James Rumsey on the Potomac River in 1786. The man had driven his boat for a few miles, it was true, but at the rate of four knots an hour. He'd never get anywhere at that speed. A good windjammer with a spanking breeze could do ten knots easily. The famous Robert Fulton, who invented the *Clermont,* had made the trip from Albany to New York, one hundred and fifty miles, in thirty hours. And he'd had a downstream current to help him, at that.

"The old busy-body should have stuck to making tea!" Stormy scoffed. Toby, who listened to his friend's tirade with patience, shook his head dubiously. He, too, preferred the clean windjammer to the dirty little steamship. He could see, however, that the latter had possibilities. He knew only too well how an owner fidgeted when a sailing vessel was becalmed in the Horse Latitudes for lack of wind. He knew how he himself had paced his widow's walk, straining to watch every speck on the horizon when a schooner was over-due after an Atlantic storm. He suspected that if the new craft could be developed properly, it might prove to be steady in any kind of weather. He said as much.

Stormalong refused to listen. He pointed to the *Savannah*. The papers were full of her crossing the Atlantic from New York to Liverpool in twenty-nine days and eleven hours. It was considered a great triumph for steam.

"Steamship?" snorted Stormalong. "The *Savannah*, as everyone knows, is an honest sailing vessel that some fool has fitted out with a pair of engines and side-paddles. She used her steam for only three and a half days out of the whole voyage. Then she gave up and did the sensible thing. She unfurled her canvas to a southwest wind!"

He paused for breath. "The *Tuscarora* cleared Boston the same day. Without any newfangled nonsense, we reached Southhampton in twenty-five days!"

Toby had to admit that Stormalong's figures were correct.

"Bah!" said Stormy with finality. "The day a teakettle bests the *Tuscarora*, Davy Jones will open his locker personally to receive my body!"

For several years the great captain continued to scoff at the tiny, puffing, coal-driven boats. They kept their place, however, and stuck to the rivers and the coastwise lanes. The open sea remained the province of the sailing vessel. Stormalong chuckled to himself as he watched the little "teakettles" ducking into the harbors. He began even to have a sort of patronizing affection for them. He went so far as to say that he might be willing to use them as tenders for loading and unloading cargo. The only difficulty he could foresee about that was that they would have to stay to leeward of the *Tuscarora,* to keep from dirtying the white paint of her hull with their filthy smoke.

While he was still considering this move, something happened which changed his amused toleration to undying hatred.

After a dense fog in the Grand Banks, the *Tuscarora* emerged into bright sunshine. Far ahead on the horizon rose a column of black smoke. The look-out in the forward crow's-nest was the first to spot it.

"Ship in distress, sir!" he sang out. "She appears to be on fire, sir! Two degrees to port, sir!"

Captain Stormalong put his glass to his eye. What he saw stirred him to action. A small two-masted vessel lay apparently drifting in the trough of the waves. Fore and aft, its sails hung limply from the yardarms, trying to pick up whatever breeze there might be. A cloud of thick, bitter smoke poured out from amidships. To a sailor there is nothing worse than the horror of a fire at sea. This burning ship seemed to be carrying a cargo of coal, from the blackness of her smoke. Her peril was great indeed! Stormalong ordered the *Tuscarora* to race to the rescue.

Immediately they reached the side of the disabled ship, Stormy's men flew to their posts. Soon all the fire hoses of the great windjammer were playing like giant fountains into the heart of the poor burning merchantman. The galley boys formed a bucket brigade to empty Porky's dishwater onto the conflagration. In no time at all, the smoke fizzled away. The little ship was saved!

When the last wisp of steam cleared from the deck of the

brave little craft, Stormy withdrew to his cabin. He washed the greasy soot from his face and combed his hair and his mustaches. He waited in proper elegance for the other captain to pay his respects and express his gratitude. No one came. Stormy went up on deck.

There, to his bewilderment, he found an angry quarrel going on. Bullfinch, his first officer, was standing at the rail, scowling. A furious little man, his captain's uniform dripping wet, was screaming and shaking his fist up at the *Tuscarora*.

"Piracy! It's piracy under any law of admiralty!" he was yelling.

Stormalong stepped quickly to the rail. "What's going on here," he asked.

The little man turned to him in fury. "Are you the master of this . . . this . . . this overgrown privateer?" he demanded, pointing to the *Tuscarora*.

Stormalong flushed at the insult. "That I am," he answered proudly.

"Permit me to introduce myself, Captain," the little man shouted sarcastically. "I am Captain Ebenezer Whitaker of the once great ship *The Great Western*. May I ask your name, sir?"

Stormy replied with his greatest dignity, "I am Captain Alfred Bulltop Stormalong, of the still great ship *Tuscarora!*" As modest as he was, he knew the effect which his name produced among deep water men. He expected Captain Whitaker to be impressed. Instead, the little man turned to his shivering first officer.

"Write that down!" he commanded.

The first officer obeyed.

Captain Whitaker then turned to Stormalong. "May I inquire, sir, why you have chosen to indulge yourself in this unprovoked attack upon an honest merchantman, flying the flag of your own country and in a time of peace?"

"Unprovoked attack?" asked Stormy, stung to the quick. "It was nothing of the kind, sir. Your miserable little ship was on fire. Thanks to our friendly intervention, *The Great Western* has been saved from a horrible fate."

"Saved?" screamed the little captain, clapping his hands to his brow. "Not saved at all! Ruined! I'll have you know, Captain Stormabob, or whatever your name is, that *The Great Western* was the finest ocean-going steamship afloat. You have just succeeded in putting her engines out of commission. Don't you recognize a modern vessel when you see it? My advice to you, sir, is to get the moss off that fuddy-dud brain of yours."

Stormalong had never before been so insulted. He pulled himself up to his greatest height.

"I regret that I have caused you inconvenience, Captain Whitaker." Icicles dripped from his voice. "I shall assign one of my lifeboats to tow you back to Boston."

Before the other captain could reply, Stormy spoke quickly to Bullfinch and retired to his cabin. Bullfinch ordered a schooner lowered to assist *The Great Western* on her homeward journey.

Stormy meanwhile brooded in his cabin. He had tried to be helpful, out of the kindness of his heart. What had he got for his pains? A scolding, and an ugly, scornful one at that, from an old woman in charge of a soup tureen! He saw, disappearing in a cloud of acrid black smoke, the fine days of the sea. Not while he, Alfred Bulltop Stormalong, was alive, would the steamship outrun the sailing vessel. He banged his fist down on the chart table. He swore that he would devote the last days of his life to prove that wind and canvas and human strength were supreme!

CHAPTER TEN

The Race with the Liverpool Packet

*W*HEN THE TUSCARORA reached her home port on the return trip, Stormalong learned to his embarrassment that Captain Whitaker had brought suit against him in Court of Admiralty. It was fortunate for Stormy that the judges of the Admiralty bench were, for the most part, old-timers. They believed in the traditions of the windjammer. They knew and respected the name of Alfred Bulltop Stormalong. They had, therefore, dismissed the case.

Toby, however, was disturbed. He visited his former shipmate aboard the *Tuscarora*. The latter was only too happy to see his old friend. He expected to pour out his indignation against the bothersome steam-driven ships. He soon learned that he was mistaken.

"Sit down, Captain!" Toby ordered, pointing to Stormy's chair and himself jumping up to the chart table, from which he could look his friend directly in the eye. "You and I have loved each other for many years. Because of this fact you must hear what I have to say, even though it may be painful. *The Great Western* has just been bought by our own line. Another steamship is in commission for us, *The Great Eastern,* which is an even more modern craft. You must promise me that you will not permit your prejudices to prevail against these ships!"

Stormalong was stunned. "Do you mean to tell me," he asked, "that the men who built the *Tuscarora* are now building *steam*ships?"

Toby answered gently. "The men who built the *Tuscarora* are dead. Their sons are now the majority owners of the line. You forget, Alfred my friend, that you and I belong to a passing generation!"

Stormalong had never been able to think of Toby as anything but a young boy! Now, in place of the mischievous lad who used to curl up in his pocket, he saw before him a forceful little man, dignified and erect, with a lined face and white side-burns, dressed in an old-fashioned frock coat. He realized with a shock that Toby had aged.

He looked at the reflection in the mirror above his own washstand. He was astonished at what he saw. The bright blue of sea water still shone out from his eyes. The skin of his face, however, had weathered to a deep wrinkled brown, like the cover of a rare old book. His own black hair was streaked with white. His mustaches were grizzled and dropped over his mouth in a tired fashion. He, A. B. Stormalong, was growing older, too! He was *not,* however, an old man!

Toby, sensing his friend's hurt, held out his hand. "So long as we both live," he said with great warmth, "you shall command the *Tuscarora!*"

Stormalong replied with the dignity of an old lion. "I thank you, friend. So long as I live, the *Tuscarora* shall remain the glory of the seas!"

Stormy kept his vow. For the next few years, although steamships were growing larger and faster, the *Tuscarora* kept her place as the fastest vessel afloat. She set new records for difficult voyages, and then promptly broke them. But still the competition from coal-driven ships could not be ignored.

The final blow, the last straw that broke Stormalong's determined patience, came to him in Southampton. He had been ordered to that port to pick up a cargo of steel rails. On the way across, he had the misfortune to be becalmed in the mid-Atlantic. Not a breath of air stirred for two days. There was nothing he could do about it. When he put in at the company wharf in the British port, there were no piles of rail lying on the dock. For a moment, Stormy was relieved, believing that his delay had not caused him to be late for the loading. The local agent came out to greet him, however, with bad news.

The merchants who had ordered the rails were anxious that they be delivered in Boston as quickly as possible. When the *Tuscarora* failed to appear to pick up the cargo at the appointed time, they had commissioned the *Liverpool Packet,* loaded the steel aboard her, and sent her off. The *Packet* was regarded as the wonder of the shipping world. She was known to do twenty knots in any kind of weather. Stormy had heard her design discussed, but he had never seen her.

This was the first time in his career that a steamship had

taken an assignment away from him. It was more than he could face. The men at the dock shook with fear when they saw the terrible expression that clouded the Captain's face. He said nothing. He clenched his fists, and the blue sea water of his eyes turned black and dangerous. He raised his cane. For a moment the agent feared that the Old Man would beat him. Stormalong, however, merely gestured to his officers to return to the ship. His men, afraid of the awful wrath which threatened to break on their heads, rushed to their stations. Stormy strode to the wheel. He took his bearings, checked his watch, and made an entry in the ship's log.

"Haul down the Blue Peter!" he roared. "Raise the anchor! Unfurl the main course! The *Liverpool Packet* cleared this port twelve hours ago. The *Tuscarora* shall beat her to Boston!"

For a time the wind was fair. With all her canvas crowded on the yards, the *Tuscarora* overtook the *Packet* as the latter chugged around the southwestern corner of Ireland. Captain Stormalong smiled grimly to himself as the windjammer passed the little steamer. For a day the sailing ship held the race, while the *Packet* dropped further and further behind. Then the wind died. The large courses of the *Tuscarora* drooped in the deadly calm. The *Packet* moved up behind her. Inch by inch the British steamer gained ground until she moved ahead.

Stormy's eyes narrowed with anger as the ugly little vessel passed the great windjammer. He could afford to hold his tongue, however. His petrels had just returned from the northeast with badly ruffled feathers. There was a gale blow-

ing up. Knowing that winds of a late summer nor'easter are as powerful as any, Stormy held his peace. The sails remained drooping from the rigging, awaiting the first breath of air. Suddenly the storm struck!

Stormalong's scowl changed to a smile like that of the sun when the force of the wind drove the *Tuscarora* through the water with the speed of a witch on a broomstick. Not even *The Flying Dutchman*, the ghost ship of the old legend, could touch her. Towering waves broke out over the prow. Stormy had vowed to overtake the *Packet*. Nothing would stop him now!

A main royal course suddenly bellied out and split with a sharp report like a cannon shot. The ship heeled over and buried her lee rail in the foaming sea.

"Lay aloft and reef the foresail!" shouted the First Mate.

Stormalong heard his cry and bellowed angrily, "We'll reef no sails on the *Tuscarora*. Rig a new main royal when there's

128

a lull in the storm. We'll ride out the gale with every stuns'l set, or my name's not Alfred Bulltop Stormalong!"

All that night the rigging screamed. The huge windjammer plunged through the mountainous waves with her lee rail under and water breaking over her bow. The masts creaked and bent under the strain. The wind howled and hissed in the darkness like a beast of prey, waiting for the kill.

A mizzenmast gave way. Stormalong had to strain to hold the *Tuscarora* on her course while the crew cut loose the rigging.

The foresails took the full brunt of the storm. One by one, they cracked and split under the fearful tension. But old Stormalong held the ship steady ahead.

Bared to the waist, he faced the fury of the storm alone at the wheel, as if this were a personal duel between them. The crew watched helplessly from the shelter of the foc's'le, stunned by the foolhardy courage of their skipper. His giant figure stood firm while towering waves broke over his back.

Just where they passed the *Liverpool Packet,* no one ever knew. When the *Tuscarora* limped around the tip of Cape Cod, Stormalong took from his pocket the ship's log on which he had made a notation in Southampton. The ship had left Southampton on Tuesday. She had been becalmed on Wednesday. The storm had hit on Thursday. It was now Saturday morning. The *Tuscarora* had crossed the main body of the Atlantic with the speed of the nor'easter in four days. That record is hard to equal even now. There was still no sign of the *Liverpool Packet* on the horizon.

Captain Alfred Bulltop Stormalong had proven his point.

A windjammer could beat any steamship on the seas. The cost, however, was too great.

The bells of all the churches from Cape Ann to Province-town rang joyfully when the *Tuscarora* was sighted. Shortly before her arrival an exhausted petrel had dropped into the home office, bringing word of the strange race that was taking place across the ocean. Toby and the board of directors of the line quickly prepared a reception for the winner. From towers and steeples flags fluttered to celebrate the occasion. When the masts of the big windjammer showed themselves over the rim of the sea, the crowds lining the shore went wild with joy.

An especially decorated schooner, carrying the line's officials, put out to meet their victorious ship. Even though the younger men disagreed with their giant captain about the merits of steam, they respected and loved him. They recog-

nized, too, the triumph he had brought to the line. Their ship had won an unbelievable race from the newest and finest of the British steamships. Toby was chosen to make the speech of welcome.

As they drew near to the *Tuscarora*, it became obvious to them all that something was wrong. Her masts were cracked and sagging. The courses hung in shreds from broken yard-arms. The lines of the rigging had snapped and were swinging in a purposeless tangle. There seemed to be little sign of life aboard. Only Bullfinch, of all the crew, was able to raise himself from the deck to acknowledge the arrival of the welcoming party. His face was ashen gray and streaked with salt. His clothes were torn to ribbons. He was unable to speak. He could merely point abaft.

In alarm Toby flew to the afterdeck. The sight that met his eyes broke his heart. Stormalong's great body lay slumped and broken beside the wheel. The giant was gasping, as though the effort to breathe were an agony. Toby stroked the huge bent head gently. Stormy opened his eyes and smiled. He tried painfully to move his lips, but no word came. He gestured feebly toward the log book which lay beside him.

A sigh wracked his whole frame. His head fell back. His body became limp. With Toby kneeling beside him, Captain Alfred Bulltop Stormalong breathed his last.

The log to which he had pointed lay open at the last notation. Through his tears, Toby read the final entry. "Arr. Boston, 0800 hours, av. speed 30 knots. Teakettle not sighted."

The flags which fluttered gaily on the shore were set at half mast as the schooner bearing the commitee and the survivors of the *Tuscarora's* crew returned to Boston harbor. The bells which had pealed with joy now tolled with sadness. Stormalong had won his last race. He and the *Tuscarora* were finished!

＊　　＊　　＊　　＊　　＊

It was not the fault of the *Liverpool Packet* or its master that Stormy had finally come to his end. The British captain was perhaps the saddest man of all when he heard of the great mariner's death. He offered to tow the *Tuscarora* to its final resting place in the Atlantic as a token of his personal respect for a worthy opponent. Out of a certain delicacy of sentiment, however, Toby declined his offer.

It was Toby, who of all men loved Stormy the most, who made the final funeral arrangements. He had the decks of the *Tuscarora* draped in black bunting. On what was left of her afterdeck, he ordered a dais to be built. Here rested the figure of her master, wrapped in a shroud made from her great main course. Four of the finest clippers of all time, the *Flying Cloud*, the *Lightning*, the *Sovereign of the Seas*, and the *Westward Ho*, were chartered to tow the magnificent hulk out of the harbor. While the bells tolled, and while the guns saluted, the *Tuscarora* and her master were taken out to sea.

Suddenly the tear-filled eyes of the mourners on the shore opened in amazement. As the *Tuscarora* neared the horizon, a miracle took place. Out of the bosom of the Atlantic Ocean rose a strange old-fashioned chariot, drawn by sea-horses. In this pearl-encrusted carriage, his right hand holding a trident, stood Neptune, the God of the Sea. He waved to the skippers of the clipper ships and motioned them out of the way. With an imperious gesture he brought into being a host of sea-nymphs who rose to the deck of the *Tuscarora*. Gently, ever so gently, with a web of golden chains, they lowered the body of the old sailor to the silver litter which Neptune had prepared. In a slow but stately rhythm, the God of the Sea proceeded out into the Atlantic. The funeral procession moved forward on its splendid way.

Behind Neptune and Stormalong's litter came the chariots of Triton and the Old Man of the Sea. Then with slow, solemn strokes followed the dolphins and the porpoises, the grampuses and the whales. Over their heads fluttered Stormalong's favorites, the homing petrels with their cousins, the sea-gulls, tagging after them. One by one, the great ships of history took the places of the clippers. The chosen

JOSHUA TOLFORD

four were the *Argo*, the ship in which Jason and his friends sought the Golden Fleece; the galley of Odysseus, that hero of Ithaca who traveled to the Pillars of Hercules on his way home from Troy; the *Victoria*, the only ship of Magellan's little fleet to finish its voyage around the world from West to East; and the warlike Viking shell in which Leif Ericson crossed the sea to Vineland in the Western Hemisphere in the Dark Ages.

These four ships took the *Tuscarora* in tow. Behind them came a strange fleet — a trio of little galleons, the *Niña*, the *Pinta*, and the *Santa Maria*, with Columbus as their admiral; the Spanish Armada and, with it, the *Golden Hind* of Sir Francis Drake; the *Mayflower*, with its complement of faithful Pilgrims, and the *Bonhomme Richard*, with John Paul Jones at the wheel. There were others, of course, too many to mention. There were also such ghostly pall-bearers as the *Flying Dutchman*, Captain Kidd's shivering ghost, and, at the end of the procession, the bleached bones of the *Lady of the Sea*, with a pale Captain Snard mourning his beloved adopted son.

By the time the procession crossed the horizon, the people of Massachusetts could see only a black thundercloud rising in the distance. They hurried home, fearful of rain.

This was no thunderhead! Davy Jones himself, standing on the surface of the ocean, had opened his locker to receive the body of his friend, Alfred Bulltop Stormalong, and the shell of the ship *Tuscarora*. The great black lid, rising into the sky, looked from a distance like a hurricane cloud.

The cavern of the locker gaped like a gigantic trough. Into it slid the whole funeral crew.

"Welcome, friend!" said Davy Jones.

The silver-wrapped body of Stormalong slid into its rightful place.

The lid clanged down!

The watchers, who remained, were relieved to see that the cloud had slipped away. They lingered, however, to listen to the strange music that came to them over the sea. It seemed to be merely the whining of the gentle easterly breeze that was blowing summer away and fall into being.

Toby, however, heard the words which the sea-nymphs and the petrels were singing:

> *"Stormy's gone, that good old man,*
> *To my way-hay Stormalong John!*
> *Stormy's gone, that good old man,*
> *To my aye, aye, aye, Mister Stormalong!"*

3 49 1